New Fiction

THE WILTING OF TIME

Edited by

Kelly Oliver

First published in Great Britain in 2005 by
NEW FICTION
Remus House,
Coltsfoot Drive,
Peterborough, PE2 9JX
Telephone (01733) 898101
Fax (01733) 313524

SB ISBN 1 85929 123 6

FOREWORD

When 'New Fiction' ceased publishing there was much wailing and gnashing of teeth, the showcase for the short story had offered an opportunity for practitioners of the craft to demonstrate their talent.

Phoenix-like from the ashes, 'New Fiction' has risen with the sole purpose of bringing forth new and exciting short stories from new and exciting writers.

The art of the short story writer has been practised from ancient days, with many gifted writers producing small, but hauntingly memorable stories that linger in the imagination.

I believe this selection of stories will leave echoes in your mind for many days. Read on and enjoy the pleasure of that most perfect form of literature, the short story.

Parvus Est Bellus.

CONTENTS

AS YE SOW!
F R Smith

To Tony Bland as he walked along fashionable Bond Street, pedestrians were but passing shadows. Being of that specie of human for whom work is an anathema, his brain was busy trying to think of a way to gain access to the world of the wealthy. So far he had met with little success.

He was passing the revolving doors of one of the exclusive stores, for which the area is justly famous, at the precise moment as an elegant young woman emerged. The result was predictable - they met, abruptly.

'I'm terrible sorry Madam ... please, allow me!' Bland bent to retrieve a fallen parcel, and as he did so, he caught sight of the attached label ... *Lady Fairgate ... 11, Ken ...* he had no time to read more - a uniformed chauffeur came to the lady's rescue.

'I'll put these in the car Madam ... Is this all?'

'Yes thank you, Bates.' She turned to Bland, 'And thank you Sir. I should have been looking where I was going.'

'Please don't apologise ... it was my fault entirely ... I ...'

'Home, Madam?' The chauffeur touched his cap.

'I think so, Bates.' Favouring Bland with a smile, the girl entered a waiting Rolls and was driven away.

Tony fairly shook with excitement. 'Lady Fairgate eh? ... This could be the day I've been waiting for ... if I play my cards right ... ? Let's find out where she lives!'

The telephone directory provided the answer, and for the next few days he haunted the location waiting for an opportunity to meet her again.

He did not have to wait for long. The Rolls Royce slid to a silent stop outside the elegant town house, and a few moments later the young woman ran towards it. Timing his approach to perfection, Tony arrived alongside at exactly the same moment as his quarry.

Raising his hat, Bland feigned surprise. 'What an extraordinary coincidence! The odds against bumping into you again like this must be astronomical ... fate seems determined to throw us together!' Tony smiled, a smile of genuine pleasure, and the young woman responded. She was flattered to have been remembered by such a handsome young man. For the moment, the chauffeur was ignored.

'Do you live around here, Mr ... ?'

'Bland - Tony Bland … and you are?' He chose to ignore the question of where he lived.

'Jill Carstairs … can I give you a lift?'

For a moment Bland was mystified … Carstairs? Then his brow cleared - she obviously preferred to use the family name. 'Yes please, a lift would be great, but only if it's not out of your way. I'm on my way to a meeting in Whitehall.'

'Hop in, it's no trouble at all.'

Bland had already set a date for their next meeting before they reached Whitehall, and in the following weeks, the couple became close. For some reason however Jill never invited him into her home - a fact which frustrated him greatly. If the inside was as elegant as the outside, it was an environment he coveted.

So the weeks passed! One evening, as they sat on a bench in the park, Tony said quietly, 'You know how I feel about you Jill … I love you so very much. I have from the first day we bumped into each other … will you marry me, Jill?'

The young woman stared into his eyes. There was an intense look in his gaze - a look of devotion, and she fell under his spell.

'Is it true Tony … you really love me … ?'

He folded her in his arms. She heard the excited pounding of his heart, but mistook the emotion which accelerated its beat.

'Love you … ? I adore you! Only once can a man say that in his lifetime, and mean it … yes my darling, I love you, and always will, but I never dreamed you could ever love me.'

'Yes my dearest, I will marry you … but …'

'How I have longed to hear you say that darling, but hardly dared think it … in anticipation however, I bought you this … do you like it?' Tony held out a ring. It was large, ostentatious, and in truth, rather vulgar, but to Jill, it was the stuff from which fairy stories are made.

'Oh Tony … it's beautiful … it must have cost the earth!'

'Nothing but the best for my darling.' He placed it on her finger and sealed their betrothal with a lingering kiss. 'I'll wait for you to name the day Jill, but please don't make me wait too long. Every minute will seem an eternity without you.'

'I won't dear, I promise,' whispered Jill.

Bland returned to his flat in a froth of excited expectancy. He was now heir apparent to a fortune, soon to take over his estates. He smiled.

Although he would not be marrying from purely honourable motives, one vow from the marriage service he would fulfil faithfully ... the 'richer or for poorer' bit ... he would most certainly be richer.

When Jill entered her home, Lady Fairgate noticed the flush on her young companion's face.

'You look very pleased with yourself my dear.'

'Oh I'm so happy Lady Fairgate. The young man I told you about has asked me to marry him ... look - we're engaged! Do you like it?' She held out her hand to show the ring.

The Lady saw the light in Jill's eyes and was happy for her, but at the same time, anxious. She thought back to their first meeting ... when her husband had died some three years earlier, she had applied to an agency for a companion, and Jill had come into her life. Although Jill was younger than she had anticipated, she had taken an instant liking to the girl, who was not only beautiful, but who radiated almost regal charm and a heart full of love and compassion. In a few weeks Lady Fairgate had come to love Jill as the child she had never had. With the revelation of her companion's engagement, the Lady was perturbed. Was she about to lose her ... ? 'Who is this man, Jill ... you haven't said much about him. When am I going to meet him?'

'I didn't like to impose ...'

'Nonsense child - your friends are always welcome, you should know that.'

Jill embraced her elderly companion. She had never known her real parents, an automobile accident had orphaned her when she was a baby, so her employer had become the mother and confidante she craved.

Lady Fairgate continued, 'What does he do for a living Jill? Is he a professional man?'

'I understand he works in the Foreign Office.'

'It sounds as if he is someone important. Why not ask him to dinner? I would like to go to Oakleas at the weekend, and I would like to see him before we go.'

'I'll ask him when I see him tomorrow evening ... oh, I know you'll just love him!'

'Well ... show me the ring, child!'

The Lady held Jill's finger, and for a second held her breath, but not in admiration. Lady Fairgate knew jewellery, and this, to her discerning eye, was nothing but a piece of vulgar junk, fit only as a prop in a pantomime. Seeing the happiness on Jill's face, however, she kept the knowledge to herself. She felt near to tears. It was evident that whoever the man was, he was not a fit person to court Jill, but what could he hope to gain by deceiving her? He could have no knowledge of her own intentions for Jill's future, so inheritance could not be the answer ... or could he be exploiting her sexual inexperience to satisfy his desires? The Lady was worried!

The next evening when Jill and Tony met, the man was clearly excited. 'I see you're wearing my ring darling - so we are now officially engaged, eh ... is it comfortable?'

'Yes darling, and I'll never take it off ... I'll wear it always.' She snuggled closer and kissed his cheek.

It had been a whirlwind romance so far, and Tony was eager to ride the wind. He was about to enter the world of the rich and famous ... a world that was there for the taking. Was this the right moment to press home his advantage ... why not? Why wait! 'Are you happy my darling?' he whispered.

'Blissfully my dearest.'

'Happy enough to marry me ... soon? You know how much I love you ... every moment away from you seems an eternity. I need you so very much my darling!'

Jill studied her companion's face. There was a tender curve to his lips ... it was too dark to see into the depths of his eyes, but his voice sounded sincere. 'Yes Tony ... but ...'

Bland interrupted, 'Good ... how about next Saturday ... is that too soon? There's no need to make it a big occasion ... I can get a special licence ... or we can elope to Gretna Green ... what do you say? Let's make it an adventure - a romantic adventure.' His smile grew wider as his enthusiasm grew. All his dreams were about to become reality.

'I'm afraid next Saturday is out of the question Tony ... I won't be here ... we shall be at Oakleas.'

'Oakleas ... ?'

'Yes dear. It's an estate Lady Fairgate owns in Shropshire.'

'You have another place in the country?' Things were getting more interesting by the minute. His smile threatened to bisect his face.

'Not me silly ... Lady Fairgate owns it. I am only a Lady's companion ... she is my employer!'

The impact of this intelligence was catastrophic. Tony's whole nervous system was paralysed - his face muscles froze in a ghastly grin ... it couldn't be true! He must have misheard! Had he been wasting his time on a blasted servant, as penniless as himself? Had his lungs been capable of expelling air, he would have screamed.

As his senses returned, he realised that this was an impasse he had to get out of - fast!

Jill sensed the tension in his body, but mistook the reason. 'Don't be disappointed darling, we will get married soon. Why not come to Oakleas with us ... we can fix a date there.'

Tony forced a croak. 'Yes ... great idea ... let's walk for a bit ... I'm getting cramp!' He had to get away, frustration was tearing him apart ... 'I'll see you tomorrow, eh?'

'I shall be helping Lady Fairgate to get ready, but come by all means - we can talk while I work.'

'I don't think so. I'll only be in the way!'

'Come to Oakleas then, and stay for the weekend. Lady Fairgate won't mind, and you know I want you with me ... say you will ... please?'

'Of course I will, I can't wait ... a weekend together ... perfect, but I'm afraid I have to leave you now ... I have some papers to vet for a meeting tomorrow ... I'll give you a ring, and you can let me have the address then. Goodbye my love!' With a hasty peck to her cheek, Tony was gone!

Back at his flat, Bland seethed. 'All that effort flanneling a bloody skivvy. Well, that's the last she'll see of me ... damn ... I thought I was on to a good thing there ... I'll have to change 'digs' in case she manages to find this place ... blast it!'

Jill lived in a froth of excitement that weekend ... waiting, hoping - praying that Bland would come, but there was no word from him, and she finally accepted that something had cropped up to force him to cancel.

As the days passed, disappointment grew into disbelief. She wrote to him daily, pouring out her heart, but there was no answer, until finally they were returned marked 'Gone Away'.

Lady Fairgate shared Jill's unhappiness. Through the offices of an influential friend at the Foreign Office, she sought an address at which

Bland could be contacted, but it transpired that Anthony Bland did not, nor ever had, worked there.

In the weeks that followed, the ache in Jill's heart gradually eased and she accepted that the one and only love in her life had left her. The truth was hard to come to terms with, but it was a fact. As she removed the so-called engagement ring from her finger and put it in a drawer in her dressing table, the last link with Tony was broken, and she put him out of her life.

In the meantime, Lady Fairgate was becoming increasingly fragile - she was fading fast!

One day her doctor called Jill to one side. 'You don't need me to tell you, Miss Carstairs, that Lady Fairgate is declining fast and cannot last for much longer. I'm afraid she is too old to benefit greatly from any additional medication, but she is in no pain ... her heart however is very weak and can fail at any time ... she refuses to leave here, so you will be the first to know when the end comes. I know you will be able to cope, but please call me at any time if you need help, and I will come at once.'

The doctor's words affected Jill deeply. She had grown very close to her employer - more than close ... she loved her!

As the days passed, the inevitability of Lady Fairgate's demise grew more evident. Jill hardly left her side, even though the Lady chided her for wasting her youth on someone merely waiting to die.

'Help me to the window seat, will you dear? I would like to look out over the gardens.'

'Are you sure you're strong enough ... you might catch cold.'

'Please Jill ... help me. I want to!' There was a smile on the old lady's face, and her eyes were bright.

Jill wrapped her employer in a blanket and half carried the wasted frame to the window before nestling it in a chair.

'Thank you dear ... I'll just sit here for a while - it's so lovely to see the trees and bushes.'

'And I'll sit with you ... is there anything I can get you?'

Lady Fairgate gripped Jill's fingers. 'I have everything I want with me ... there is nothing or anyone else I need ...' Her grip tightened, surprisingly strong for one so frail ... 'I love you Jill ... thank you for all you have done to make my life so happy. Kiss me child ... please ...

I ...' The voice trailed to a whisper and expired in a sigh. The Lady's head slipped onto Jill's shoulder, the tender smile still on her lips.

Jill did not have to be told Lady Fairgate had said 'goodbye'. Settling the body comfortably in the chair, she called the doctor.

She was devastated by her employer's death. Suspecting she was now redundant, she sought the advice of the family lawyer, only to be told to be patient and carry on as usual ... the Lady's wishes for her future would be disclosed at the reading of the will.

It would be difficult to describe Jill's reaction on learning that everything the Lady possessed had been left to her, with only one proviso ... the administration of the estate was to continue as before, and that those staff members who wished to do so, could remain in their jobs. The only difference therefore was that instead of Lady Fairgate being at the helm, it was Jill Carstairs.

In London meanwhile, Tony Bland continued with his precarious lifestyle. It was a parasitic existence - by leeching on to some frustrated female seeking an extra-marital experience he was reasonably well looked after, but such relationships were by their very nature often only bed and breakfast affairs. He was ever the optimist however - his outlook being 'love 'em and leave 'em' - there are plenty more fish in the sea.

A display of press photographs in the window of a provincial newspaper agency came under his idle scrutiny ... suddenly his breath hissed through his teeth ... 'I know that woman ... it's Jill ... what the hell is her picture doing here?'

Inside the agency, he bought a copy of the relevant issue. The headlines blurred before his fevered gaze ... 'Real life Rags to Riches' ... 'Orphan girl companion to Millionairess inherits one of Britain's most prestigious estates'.

His head swam. Was it possible he had missed the opportunity of a lifetime? Concentrating all his energies, he tried to think of some way to retrieve his position in Jill's life - to find some plausible excuse for his long absence. He looked at the date of the paper ... it was over three months old ... and he had broken off his engagement to Jill some two years earlier ... so, if he met her again now, he could not be accused of opportunism.

In the following days, story after story born of tortuous imagination revolved in his brain until he settled on one which might be considered feasible.

With a confident spring in his step, he arrived at Jill's country mansion and rang the doorbell.

'I've come to see Miss Carstairs,' he said breezily to the servant who answered the ring and entered without waiting.

'Is Miss Carstairs expecting you Sir?'

'Of course ... I'm her fiancé ... Tony Bland.'

'I'm afraid she is out just now Sir ...'

'Oh that's all right, I'll wait ... in the meantime, perhaps you'll tell Lady Fairgate I'm here ... don't look so surprised man - she knows me well, but it's been a long time since I saw her last ... I've been away you see ... government business!'

'Lady Fairgate died some time ago Sir - you must have ...'

Bland affected shock. 'Oh my God, I am sorry. My mission overseas was secret you see ... it wasn't possible to write or receive correspondence ... I only got back a couple of days ago ... had I known, I would have ...' He paused ... 'This is rather embarrassing. I brought along a few things expecting to stay at least for the night, but perhaps it would be better if I stayed in a hotel ... can you recommend ...'

'I'm sure that won't be necessary Sir. Miss Carstairs will not be long, and there are plenty of spare rooms. If you will follow me, you will be comfortable in the drawing room. May I get you a drink?'

'Thanks ... scotch and soda please ... I must say, this news has shaken me up ... difficult to take in!' With his clipped speech, Tony hoped to give the impression of a secret agent.

When the butler had left, Bland took note of his surroundings. His mask of pseudo sadness dropped and his eyes shone with appreciation. Luxury fit for a millionaire it was indeed! And it all belonged to Jill and in a little while, if he hadn't lost his touch - to him. There would be difficulties with Jill at first over his lengthy absence, but if he couldn't win her back, he was not the man he was.

He helped himself to another drink, and settled back to enjoy his dream.

It was not long before Jill returned. There was no welcoming smile on her face however, but Bland appeared not to notice. He advanced towards her with outstretched arms.

'Hullo sweetheart - I'm back! These last years away have been Hell darling ...'

'What do you want Tony ... why are you here?'

'Why ... ? I've come back home ... I've been away ...'

'So you have, and you didn't even trouble to let me know. When my letters were returned, my heart nearly broke ... I loved you then Tony, and you left me without a word.'

'I didn't desert you darling. When I got home after our last date, I received orders to leave at once for ...'

Jill interrupted. 'You told me you worked for the Foreign Office, but Lady Fairgate checked, and they had never heard of you.'

'Well they had to say that, didn't they darling? Secret Intelligence demands it. I couldn't tell you - neither could they without compromising my cover. On a mission, an agent is on his own.'

'You ... in Intelligence?' There was a hint of mockery in Jill's tone. 'Why are you telling me now in that case?'

'I am no longer engaged on sensitive activities, though I am still sworn to secrecy of course. It was sheer hell where I was Jill - the only thing which kept me going was the thought of you.' Bland again tried to take her in his arms ... 'I love you Jill darling - I always have, and always will. We have wasted too much time ... can't we just get back to how things were?'

Jill backed away. 'I'm afraid that's not possible Tony. A lot has happened since I saw you last. By the way, how did you know where to find me?'

'The caretaker at the London house told me. I was shocked to hear she had passed away ... what will you do now Jill? Looking for a new job, no doubt!'

'I don't need to look for a job now, Tony.'

'Of course you don't dear. I'll take care of you, and after we're married, there'll be no more drudgery for you my love.' Moving to the decanter he poured a drink ... 'Oh sorry my darling, can I get you one?'

Jill shook her head. Bland stared at her hand.

'I see you're not wearing my ring ... frightened of losing it eh? Oh, by the way, the butler hinted I might stay here for a while ... can you arrange it, do you think?'

'I should be able to, I own the place.'

Bland tried to look surprised. 'How do you mean?'

'Everything you see is mine, Tony - the house - its contents - the grounds - farms ... absolutely everything!'

'Wow! ... Everything ... ? I can't believe it! Why ... ?'

'I really don't know ... I was all she had, I suppose.'

'How on earth will you manage? It's a large estate by the look of it ... you'll need help.' He paused, then ... 'But that's no problem ... that's where I come in ... I can ...'

'You are wrong, Tony, that's where you don't come in. Do you think you can walk back into my life after all this time and just take over? Oh no, Tony, you hurt me far too much for that.'

'But I have explained my darling ... maybe a man in my profession ought not to fall in love, but that is a human's right, isn't it? We were so happy Jill - so perfectly suited ... we are still the same couple, aren't we? We have both suffered through unavoidable circumstances, but we can put all that behind us now. I want to marry you Jill, and take care of you ... just devote my life to you. Please ...'

He was interrupted by a discreet knock at the door ... 'Mr Rogers has arrived Madam. I have shown him into the study.'

Bland noticed the sparkle in Jill's eyes and its meaning was obvious ... she fancied another man!

'Thanks James. Tell him I'll not be long.' She turned to Tony. 'I'm sorry, I have to go out. I don't know when I'll be back, but if there is anything you want, just ask James.'

'But Jill, I ...'

'Goodbye Tony!' Without a backward glance, she left.

From a window, Bland watched Jill and her escort cross to a car and drive away. The man's arm had been around Jill's waist, and there was not the slightest doubt they were close. He bit his lip ... she had a lover! The prospect of letting slip all this wealth was unthinkable. Somehow he had to prolong his stay, and persuade this other man to quit ... but how to achieve it?

He rang the servant's bell ... 'Ah James - can you rustle me up something to eat? A sandwich will do, and something to wash it down.'

'Certainly Sir. I'll send it up to your room, or would you prefer a tray here?'

'Here will do fine.'

'Very good Sir ... after you have eaten, if you prefer to read, there is a fine library here - or perhaps you would like to walk in the grounds - the foliage is particularly colourful at this time of the year.

'Don't worry about me James, I'll find something to do.'

As he explored the house and gardens, he tried to assess their value, and caught his breath ... it had to be enormous! Surely there was some way to ensure it came to him. If only he could get Jill on her own for sufficient time, he was sure he could play on her sentimentality and win her over. He remembered how sensitive she was. She couldn't have changed all that much! If only he could get her to listen ... he would tell her of his sufferings in some imagined hell-hole, unable to break cover ... with enemy agents all around ... with only the thought of his love for her to sustain him ... given the opportunity he could put on an act fit for a Shakespearean tragedy ... if only he could get her to listen!

As he concentrated, he began to believe the story being born in his mind ... his eyes closed and his breathing quickened ... he was being pursued by implacable hunters ... crawling belly down in a tangle of jungle undergrowth ... running ... streaming with sweat until - cornered at last, he rounded on his pursuers to battle for his life ... machine pistol spitting, he watched them fall ... guns were blazing ... there was an excruciating pain in his leg and a groan broke from his lips.

'Are you all right, Sir?' The solicitous voice of Jill's butler cut through his returning consciousness.

The pain in Tony's leg was real - it was a cramp. He must have fallen asleep on the sofa. Rubbing his eyes, he replied, 'Sorry James, I must have dropped off ... nasty dream! I get them sometimes. I had some bad moments on my last mission, and they take a long time to get over.'

'I'm sure they do, Sir. Would you care for another drink?'

'Yes please ... have you any idea when Miss Carstairs will be back?'

'She will be here for dinner, Sir. We dine at seven.'

Jill returned soon after six. 'Did you manage to find something to occupy you? I'm sorry I had to leave so abruptly, but I had urgent business to attend to.'

Bland assumed an injured air. 'No Jill, I did not have an enjoyable time. It was a wasted afternoon as far as I was concerned. Without you darling I …'

'Please don't be tiresome Tony. What we had was good while it lasted, but it was a long time ago … things have changed … I have changed. My life is completely different now. I have other interests and responsibilities … other friends.'

'Like that chap you were with today!'

'Yes - like the chap I was with today.' Jill was angry.

Bland decided to try his Othello act. 'Forgive me darling, I didn't mean to criticise, but I'm jealous … you can understand, can't you? I've been through Hell, and I've suffered loneliness and pain … only the thought of you …'

It was Jill's turn to interrupt. 'Please don't go on, Tony. There was a time when I would have believed you … but now, I'm sorry, I'm just not interested.'

'But if we love each other …'

'We do not love each other, Tony. I did love you once, with all my heart, but I learned long ago it was a one-sided affair … you never loved me. You mistook me for someone I was not.'

'That's not true … I did love you … I still do. You accepted my ring as a token of our engagement - remember … does that mean nothing to you now?'

Jill smiled wryly. 'Oh the ring … yes, of course. I will let you have it back, Tony. You may find it useful in the future. You'll see that the metal has gone black and the stone doesn't sparkle anymore … it's just a worthless piece of junk, but I'm sure you knew that when you gave it to me.'

'I didn't … I swear. I paid …'

'Spare me the details Tony, I don't want to know - and I don't think I want you at my dinner table, your conversation bores me. I'll have a tray sent to your room. You may stay here for the night, but I expect you to be gone tomorrow. Goodbye Tony, for the last time, and I mean, the last time!'

'No … you can't leave me like this Jill - not after all we have been to one another … you must give me another chance.' His tone changed to a menacing rumble … 'There's someone else, isn't there?'

'Since you ask, although you have no right to ... there is someone else, and in a couple of months we are to be married.'

Tony was shattered, his dreams were in ruins. Frustration turned to anger. 'I hope your promises to him mean more than they did for me ... see how loyal he can be ... I only managed to stay alive because of your promise to me ... it was all that kept me going ... but it wasn't the same for you, was it? Well, you're free to play the field now I suppose ... I hope you enjoy each other!'

The woman was unimpressed. 'Goodbye, Tony!'

Later, as he lay on his bed, a thousand schemes ran through Tony's brain - dark, turbulent thoughts, but all reaching for the same conclusion. If he could not have Jill, then no one else would ... !

But that would mean removing his rival ... for a moment his mind rebelled. To call upon the services of The Reaper would command a high fee! A poem he had once read came to mind, and a shiver ran through him ... 'What the Devil buys with Devil's pay - the Devil is sure to hold!' An imp had already lodged in his mind however ... would not all of this wealth be worth it?

Bland breakfasted early next morning and left. His plan of action had matured. Unlike Achilles who brooded in his tent however, Tony brooded in the open throughout the whole of that long day, waiting for his rival.

Evening came - it was dark and wet. Drizzle was turning to sleet, but Bland was oblivious to the weather - he waited patiently in the lee of a dry-stone wall.

Eventually Jill's fiancé arrived, and a malignant smile curved Tony's lips ... 'And the condemned man ate a hearty breakfast, or dinner, as the case might be,' he muttered evilly.

Sliding beneath the man's car, he cut through the brake lines, and resumed his position opposite the entrance to the driveway. He seemed impervious to the cold, and lit a cigarette in cupped hands ... his nerves tingled with excitement and anticipation.

Outside the driveway gates, the road descended in a sharp decline towards the valley, twisting and turning in a series of difficult bends. The road was coated with icy slush ... Bland's breath exhaled in a hiss as the lovers appeared in the doorway. He squirmed as he watched them embrace ... then he laughed, an eerie sound, lost in the surrounding gloom.

'Be careful, darling!' called Jill as her fiancé engaged the gears.

'Yes - do be careful darling!' mocked Bland as he eagerly took up a position opposite the gates to give a grandstand view of the road.

He laughed aloud as the car left the drive and turned onto the road … he could see the driver wrestling with the steering wheel, and imagined his fear as he stabbed at the unresponsive brakes …

Tony was laughing uncontrollably as he watched … laughter which froze on his lips as the vehicle spun on the ice and hurtled towards him.

He just had time for one horrified scream before he was crushed against the dry-stone wall.

So ended Bland's dream of sharing Jill's inheritance … he did benefit in a small way however … Jill paid for his funeral!

WHAT'S IN THE STARS?
Marian Bythell

You could sum Edward up in one word, or rather two. He was 'a plodder!' Faithful, steady, reliable, hardworking and he'd been at T Cavendish & Sons Ltd, Insurance Agents so long that he seemed part of the furniture.

Frances sipped her coffee thoughtfully. It wasn't an official tea break but she was so fed up of routine office work, staring at the computer, she wanted fun.

Edward was a quiet type. He was earnestly looking at his computer, tapping away on the keyboard rhythmically, answering the phone patiently. But what else did she know about him? He was single, that was true, as she was, but was he looking for love? She supposed he was what you'd call the eternal bachelor. She liked his shy profile, his neat brown hair and deep brown spaniel eyes framed in black spectacles.

Frances trailed her fingers through her long blonde hair and eyed the other occupants. Sally, the office junior, was painting her nails. Barry, computer whizz kid and office flirt was sleek and single, but definitely not her type. John, behind the big desk, was solid and sociable, but married.

Frances kept her eye on Edward and decided it was time to break the noise of clattering keyboards. She got up, taking her notebook with her and leaned over Edward's shoulder. He looked up enquiringly.

'I'm doing a survey Edward and wondered when your birthday is?'

'Why?' He looked startled.

'Well, I believe in compatibles.' Frances jumped in at the deep end. 'You must know about that. Star signs. I'm a Pisces. They are daydreamers and I go with Cancer and Scorpio.'

'Oh, you don't believe in that stuff,' he replied.

'Oh, it seems proven. My best friend at school was a Cancer star sign - July 12th. It's the same with men and women relationships.'

Edward looked embarrassed.

'Look, I've not time to discuss this now,' he hesitated. 'How about a spot of lunch together?'

Frances' heart fluttered. 'Of course.' (Did that mean he was compatible? She regarded him thoughtfully as she picked up a pile of mail needing to be dealt with. He didn't fit in with any of her theories about Cancer and Scorpio. Cancer were moody, hid in their shells but were also very friendly. Scorpio were psychic and had a 'sting' in their tail, or so Mum told her, but they were both water signs like her own.)

They ate at Luccis Italian Restaurant, Edward insisted on paying for their meal. He refused to talk about her 'survey' until after dessert and they sipped steaming cappuccinos contentedly.

Frances was eager for him to talk about star signs. She leaned forward, her hair tumbling about her shoulders. Were they compatible? Well, they always got on well with each other.

'Right Frances, now what's all this about?'

'It's just that my parents are desperate for me to find the right man. They're old fashioned you see and well, I thought I'd follow the stars!' She was babbling on and he interrupted her.

'Star signs! No, it's nonsense. It's personalities that count. It's what's in here!' and he banged his chest.

'Oh you mean the soul,' she answered quietly, but then added, 'but what's yours; when's your birthday?'

'April 23rd.'

'Oh, you're a Taurus, on the cusp,' she said disappointedly. (Well, that figures she thought, he really was laid back!)

They finished their meal in silence. Frances' shoulders drooped and Edward looked concerned, then he spoke up.

'Look here, did you say Cancer was June or July? My brother's birthday is June 28th. He's staying with me at the moment on leave from the navy. Would you like to meet him?'

Frances leapt at the chance. She'd always liked Edward and David, his younger brother seemed most inviting.

A week later, Frances regarded Edward as he tapped away on the computer. David turned out to be ten years younger than herself and naïve, and when they were in the cinema together, he'd gone really quiet on her, gone into his shell! They hadn't even exchanged a kiss.

Frances was hugely embarrassed about the whole episode and confronted Edward over coffee break.

'I'm sorry about David,' she blurted out.

'So am I. You look so young, I thought he was nearer your age. Now it seems you and I were born the same year. We're both 30 and we could have been in the same class as school except we were born in different counties!'

Frances giggled. He really was a dear.

'Listen Frances, I've an idea. Let's have lunch at Luccis again.'

Frances readily agreed.

Over lunch, he gave her a list of his friends, friends he'd known at school or his business life.

'I don't want a date with Barry from work,' she insisted.

The next few weeks were a whirl of activity. She was introduced to Joseph, a farmer from a village several miles away; Richard who was an insurance agent from a firm known to theirs; Stephen, an engineer and Colin a statistics expert.

It seemed none of these were Cancer or Scorpio or even Pisces like herself but what had Edward said, 'It was your personality that counted.' But none of them brought any fun to her life.

Three months later, Frances looked at the desk where Edward usually sat. It had been replaced by Richard who had left his insurance agents' firm to work for theirs. But where was Edward? Frances busied herself all morning feeling disappointed that Edward wasn't there to talk to as usual and he hadn't told her where he had gone. He had been out of the office for over a week. She thought they were firm friends.

That evening her mum rang her.

'Met any nice men lately?'

Frances started crying and told her mum about the last few weeks.

'And where's Edward?' was all her mum could say trying to sound sympathetic.

Frances didn't know. Her mum suggested she should ring him. Perhaps he had another list of friends.

Luckily he was in. Yes, he'd been busy and visiting relatives, including his brother David. No, he had run out of friends who were unattached but he did know of one man who was very interested in her and would she consider dating him? Yes, he was her own age and free. Yes, he repeated. He was very interested in her.

Frances said, 'What's his name?'

'Edward,' replied Edward.

'Oh Edward, that's the best idea you've had yet,' sighed Frances.

LISSETTE
Ivy Allpress

They sat along the branches and in the thicket waiting expectantly, bright eyes and sharp beaks at the ready.

Spring, summer, autumn, winter, in all seasons they waited, on the bare twigs in winter and hidden in the leafy bushes in the summer.

She was late, where was she? A marauding cat caused a flutter and broke the silence, but he passed by, seeking other quarry.

One of the bolder spirits flew to the ground and was soon joined by some friends. They grubbed about in yesterday's remainders, now dry and unappetising.

A blackbird sounded a warning note. It was probably Hodgkin who belonged to the house. Loud and urgent was the blackbird's call. They flew to the safety of the trees.

A pair of wood pigeons, plump and sleek waited on a nearby roof, the early morning sun picking out the iridescent feathers round their necks. Would she come? She always did - rain, hail, snow or blow.

There was a sharp sound, the latch was being lifted, the back door opened and two brown dogs rushed out, barking noisily. She was walking down the path carrying a basket full of crusts, biscuits and cake crumbs which she scattered on the lawn, and calling the dogs went back into the house.

When all was quiet once more the birds came down and proceeded to demolish the feast. Some flew off carrying morsels in their beaks for their waiting families. Others ate where they stood until satisfied. Then a sudden movement of curtains at the back of the house caused them to fly up to the protection of the trees until tomorrow morning when the question would be - would she come?

Yes she would come tomorrow, nothing was surer than that, so ordered had her life become. But it was not always so. She paused before a portrait of herself as she walked back to the comfortable chintzy living room. Memories came flooding back. She saw before her a young girl, fresh faced and lovely, but somewhat pensive looking leaning against an old chair. Her soft brown hair flowed freely and her floral dress hung gracefully round her shoulders and slender figure, one slim hand clasping the necklace at her throat.

Did I really look like that? she wondered.

A discerning observer would have noticed that basically she had changed very little. The process of ageing sat lightly on her. A little plumper perhaps, a slight greying of the brown hair, but discreetly tinted, and the inevitable stress lines that come with life's problems but her skin was fresh and clear and her eyes were still bright if still a little pensive.

Madame Skortsky ran the dancing academy like a regiment. A tall dignified woman, straight backed like a ramrod with snow white hair piled high. She came from somewhere in Eastern Europe, but liked to give the impression that she was an exiled Russian aristocrat.

A strict disciplinarian, she was an excellent teacher of ballet and the little girls who were accepted by her as pupils could consider themselves extremely lucky.

Such a one was Lissette. Her home was comfortable but modest. Her father was a hardworking master builder running his own small business. Her mother was a good housekeeper but very keen on the arts and given to flights of fancy. Hence the dancing and piano lessons and the name Lissette. Her older brothers laughed at her name and called her Lizzie. She did not mind however, she was a good tempered little girl who took life as it came.

The dancing class was the high spot of her life. She was terrified of Madame and obeyed her implicitly. She wanted only to please her and she worked hard and long. Madame recognised her potential and helped to develop it.

On her sixteenth birthday Lissette was told that her hard work had been rewarded. She had been given a place in the corps de ballet of a well known company. She was overjoyed. She wanted to throw her arms around Madame and hug her but she did not dare.

Shivering in the chilly changing room after working hard at the bar she was aware of the envious glances of some of the other pupils. However most of them were friendly and pleased at her success.

Their turn will come, she thought. After all Madame had many successful pupils, after all she was starting on the bottom rung of a very steep ladder.

Madame was talking to someone as the girls filed out of the academy. A tall distinguished looking man somewhat saternine in appearance. He had a greying forked beard and piercing dark eyes which followed Lissette as she walked out of the building.

'Did you see who was talking to Madame?' asked Anna her best friend at the class.

'I saw a man, but who is he? He looks a bit alarming,' Lissette replied.

Anna came from a Bohemian background and considered herself very worldly and superior. 'It's Anton Greville the famous painter, he's a friend of Madame's.'

'Oh,' said Lissette, not at all impressed. Her mind was on the corps de ballet and how she would fit in.

The girls stepped out into the crisp, wintry air. The bare trees made black patterns against the clear blue sky. Such delicate traceries no lace maker could ever hope to copy and the little dark bobbles on the end of the twigs were like festoons on a Christmas tree. Christmas! It would soon be Christmas and rehearsals for the academy's production of the 'Nutcracker' were in full swing. The morning's hard work had made the girls hungry. They were just going to turn into their favourite cafe when Anna noticed the famous artist pass them. He lifted his hat in brief recognition and passed on his way, but Lissette was suddenly aware of his deep penetrating eyes again and she shivered slightly and felt glad of the warmth of the busy restaurant.

Madame's production of the 'Nutcracker' was a great success and Lissette's Sugar Plum Fairy was a dream. Her parents were so proud of her and even her brothers applauded.

After the performance a party was given for the people concerned with the production and their families were invited as well. A huge Christmas tree was wheeled on the stage with presents for everybody. The performers still wore their costumes which added sparkle to the colourful scene. Lissette and Anna flitted about from guest to guest, handing round drinks and refreshments. Lissette was very excited with it all. Her cheeks were flushed and her eyes bright and suddenly she found herself standing in front of Madame's artist friend, looking into his strange dark eyes. To say that she was disconcerted was to put it mildly.

Madame came to her rescue. 'Ah Anton,' she said, 'I want you to meet my brightest pupil.'

'Charmed,' said the man and bent and kissed her hand. 'I must congratulate you on your dancing.'

Madame went on to explain how she was going to join the ballet company in the new year and the artist declared he was going to look out for her performances.

This was all heady stuff for a girl like Lissette who had always been sheltered and she was glad to make her escape as soon as she decently could.

Anna grabbed her at once. 'What did he say to you? He's very famous and important you know.'

'He said he liked my dancing, that's all.' Lissette suddenly felt very tired and looked for her parents, she just wanted to go home.

Christmas came and went and the new year dawned. The time had come to enter the real world. Gone forever was the protection of the dancing academy. Work in the ballet company was hard and exacting but rewarding. Many times Lissette had reason to be thankful for the discipline that lessons with Madame had taught her. Her fellow dancers in the company were kind and helpful to her as a newcomer and Lissette began to make progress.

One day she noticed someone sitting at the back of the theatre sketching. She thought the figure looked familiar and on closer inspection she discovered that it was Madame's artist friend. Again she felt a strange uneasy feeling, she could not explain it. It was like a queer sort of excitement, the artist looked up and met her gaze.

'Hello Lissette,' he said, his strange eyes lighting up with pleasure.

'I have been watching your career, and I am making some sketches for a series of lectures I am giving on art and the ballet, come and see.'

She looked at the folder of sketches of the company and was amazed at how he had caught the spirit of what they aimed for in their work.

'They are lovely,' she explained, 'they are exactly right, it's just how we are.'

'Of course,' he answered, 'the ballet is one of my greatest loves and drawing the dancers my greatest pleasure.'

Lissette thought that this was a perfect answer and hurried back to rehearsals feeling in a whirl and delighted that she figured in so many of the sketches.

He was waiting for her at the stage door at the end of practice and asked her to lunch. She accepted because she could not think of an excuse not to, but found that she enjoyed his company. He knew so much about everything. Her own world was narrowly confined to the ballet and it was stimulating to hear about so many interesting things.

They stepped out into the wintry sunshine. There was quite an edge on the wind, which was seeing off the last of the leaves still clinging to the gaunt trees which lined the street. The wind was triumphant and the leaves went swirling and dancing along the pavement.

Everything looked so much sharper and more clearly defined to Lissette. The slate grey of the roof tops with bright red chimney pots were stretched against the skyline like soldiers. The gulls had arrived wheeling and crying, looking for shelter from the storms and privations of the coast. Lissette wished she had some bread for them as they settled on the green, bright eyed, with hooked beaks - fierce looking, rather like her companion.

They continued down the busy street. The world and his wife were traversing down. Along the road sped the red buses, fire engines and GPO vans, contrasting with the white ambulances and black taxis, all aspects of human life seemed to be manifesting and the clamour was deafening.

The artist took her back to the theatre where rehearsals were in full swing for the Christmas productions. Christmas again! How the year had flown. It had nearly gone full circle to the time of her joining the ballet company. It had been a happy and fulfilling time until today when she felt both elated and frightened.

It was in the new year that Anton Greville proposed that she should sit for a portrait for him. Her father was dead against the idea. His forthright opinions of artists could not be repeated. Her mother was thrilled however, this was the art world she had always dreamt about. It was decided that her mother should accompany her to the studio which was situated on the top floor of a recently restored Georgian house.

The pose for the portrait was most uncomfortable. She had to lean against an antique chair one arm supporting her chin, the other resting on the back of the chair.

The dress provided for her to wear was beautiful, made of pure silk with pastel shaded flowers printed all over and a pearl and gold necklace completed the ensemble. Her hair was brushed free and flowing from the tight ballerina bun, and there were tiny pearl earrings in her ears.

By this time she was absolutely fascinated by the artist and willingly suffered the agony of the cramp and pain posing for the portrait inflicted on her. It was almost like her early ballet lessons with Madame, when she had been willing to suffer anything to please her. The artist began to escort her to various social functions in the art world. His behaviour towards her was always correct, almost paternal, and she seemed like a little dog trotting behind him. She was still working hard in the ballet company. He encouraged her in this.

Then came the day for the portrait to be exhibited. It was an overwhelming success and Lissette found herself to be a celebrity overnight. People wanted to know who she was and where she came from. The media wove such fantastic stories about her that Lissette had a job to recognise herself.

It was all very exciting but it was an unreal world she found herself in and she did not really like it. She would never have coped with it without the support and guidance of Anton Greville. He revelled in public adulation. It was all part of his scheme of things, this dazzling fairy world with himself as the great man and she as his little disciple.

As she moved in more elevated circles she found that the artist had a following of devoted admirers. This did not stop her adoration of him. He was her friend, her mentor, her educator and she could not visualise life without him, although she was still afraid of him especially his eyes, dark, piercing, not gentle they seemed to be searching for her very soul. Lissette's dancing career progressed and she became a celebrity in her own right and no longer bathed in the reflected glory of the portrait which had become quite famous. She had many admirers, quite a band of devotees, but no one in her life had the same effect on her as Anton Greville, sometimes she wished that she could be free of his influence, she felt that she was never herself. He seemed to sense her unease and suggested another portrait, something different, more modern. She agreed and was making her way to the studio one lunchtime when she noticed the placards by the news stand, 'Famous artist killed'.

Her heart turned to stone. She knew who it must be. With trembling hands she bought a paper from the news boy.

'Are you alright Miss?' he asked anxiously.

'Perfectly,' she replied and quickly turned and glanced at the paper.

Yes it was all there. The horrific details of the accident and also that his wife and family were returning from the south of France where they had been living. Wife and family, he had never mentioned them. She had stupidly supposed that he had no one else in his life. Lissette was utterly desolated. Her world had turned upside down and shattered, she felt so cold she was sure she would never be warm again. She was numb inside.

The day of the funeral arrived and many distinguished people from all walks of life were gathering for the event. Lissette kept to the back of the church hardly seeing or hearing anything. She hated all the publicity surrounding such a tragic happening. She followed on to the cemetery keeping well out of sight. When it was all over she turned to go but felt a hand on her arm. She found she was looking up into another pair of dark eyes, but these were kind and gentle.

'You must be Lissette,' said the owner of them. 'I'm Tony Greville, Anton's son, please come back to the house with us. My father thought such a lot of you, you reminded him of my sister who died. He had such plans for her and you took her place a little.'

She suffered herself to be led along, she just felt cold and sick and tears were running down her cheeks.

He led her to a large comfortable house nearby. She felt utterly bewildered, there was so much she did not know. Inside the warm room she relaxed a little and noticed some of her celebrated acquaintances. Tony introduced her to his younger brothers John and Peter, and then led her over to meet his mother. She was a plump, pretty woman of middle years who told her that after their daughter had died she and Anton had drifted apart, each following their own careers, she was a writer, and in fact had not seen him for years. The boys kept in touch with their father though.

Lissette's friendship with Tony Greville flourished and inevitably they fell in love and married. Tony became a lawyer of some distinction and they bought a pleasant house with a large rambling garden.

Lissette left the ballet to have a family, four children in fact, and had no desire to resume her career. She felt settled at last. Now for the first time in her life she had no one to dominate her. She could be herself and she loved the predictability of her well ordered life.

Spring, summer, autumn, winter and spring again, the birds would be waiting. Would she come to feed them? They knew she would.

MICHELLE AND DAVE'S STORY
Louise Caroline Wheeler

It was almost seven thirty. He would be arriving any minute. Michelle took one last look at herself in the hall mirror. She and Dave had known each other for years and had become close friends after both their recent divorces. For some reason, she couldn't understand why, Michelle was feeling very nervous.

'You idiot,' her reflection told her, 'you are 32 years old, Dave is just a friend who has asked you to go out for a meal as friends. It's no big deal.'

'Then why am I feeling like a teenager about to go on her first date?' Michelle asked.

'You're pathetic,' her reflection laughed.

There was a knock at the back door.

'Hello, I'm ready,' Michelle said brightly as she opened it.

Dave stood there looking very smart in a dark blue jacket and tie.

'Very nice,' he said smiling appreciatively at Michelle's blue dress and matching sandals.

As they got into the car Dave gave Michelle a single white rose. 'White for friendship,' he smiled. Michelle's stomach gave a little flutter as she placed the rose on the back seat of the car. They had a lovely drive to the restaurant down leafy country lanes, chatting about this and that, relaxed and comfortable in each other's company although Michelle was still feeling nervous.

World's End was a typically English style country restaurant with leaded windows and roses round the door. It had an intimate cosy atmosphere and was filled with couples enjoying a romantic night out.

Michelle and Dave were shown to a secluded table in the corner where they ordered their meal. After a while Michelle looked at Dave and shook her head slightly.

'What's wrong?' asked Dave looking concerned, 'don't you like it?'

'Oh yes,' replied Michelle, 'I was just wondering why you would want to go to all this trouble for me? I mean I'm nothing special, just your sensible friend,' that was a private joke between them, 'so why?'

Dave didn't know how to answer this rather unnerving question and he gave a sigh of relief as the arrival of dessert meant he didn't have to. Over coffee the conversation returned to normal and afterwards the couple left the restaurant and returned to the car where Dave presented Michelle with another single rose but this time it was red.

'Red to say thank you for a lovely evening,' he said quietly.

Michelle was caught totally unawares so she just smiled nervously and placed it on the back seat with the white one. As the car moved into the lane Michelle began to have a conversation in her head.

'Did Dave want to be more than friends? No of course not, he was just being a gentleman. But what if he does, what do I do? Oh, for goodness sake just grow up and enjoy the drive home.'

The journey home was taken in companionable silence as each of them drifted off into their own thoughts. All too soon the car arrived on Michelle's drive.

'Thank you for a wonderful evening,' said Michelle as she reached for her roses.

'The pleasure was all mine,' Dave answered quietly. 'Maybe we could do it again sometime.'

'I'd like that,' Michelle replied as she opened the car door and moved to step out.

'Michelle!'

Michelle turned her head and Dave leant forward quickly and placed a small kiss on her lips. Time stood still as Michelle stared, wide eyed with surprise at Dave.

'I'm sorry,' he said, 'I shouldn't have done that.'

'No don't be sorry, I'm just surprised that's all. It certainly changes things. I don't really know what to say.'

Dave leant forward again and kissed her goodnight properly this time. It was a slow, gentle, loving kiss which left Michelle's senses reeling.

'Oh, Michelle if you only knew how long I've waited for this moment. The times you said that you were nothing special and to me you are the most perfect woman in the whole world. You also said that nobody else would want you and I just wanted to shout *I do!'*

'I'd better go,' Michelle whispered, 'I'll see you soon.' She got out of the car and disappeared down the driveway to her back door. After closing the door behind her she leant against it, holding the roses close to her heart, and closed her eyes. Her heart was beating madly in her chest and her face was on fire.

Oh help, she thought, *now what do I do?*

STARTING OVER
John Robinson

I guess I keep picking the wrong women. They seem like the right ones at the time but my track record suggests otherwise! Or maybe I've picked the right one a few times, but somehow managed to let her go.

The 'love of my life' is still the one I met at seventeen. My 'Girl of Brigadoon'. She feels the same. I know, because she has told me many times over the intervening years. She quite recently introduced me to members of her family as 'My Childhood Sweetheart' for God's sake, but it wasn't to be. I don't recall what got in the way, maybe we were too young, maybe I was too wild, whatever. But she's always there, in my thoughts and in my heart.

Then there was another, who could have been something special. Again I don't really know what went wrong. I actually bumped into her just a couple of weeks ago and she asked me, 'What happened between us?'

I replied that I didn't know, but that it was one of my biggest regrets. She told me she'd had a decent life with a good bloke but that she always felt that I was the one for her. C'est la vie.

Then I got married. We travelled the world, had some pretty good times and eventually had two wonderful children. For a good few years we were a perfect family. Then I suppose we drifted apart, developed different desires and ambitions and eventually divorced. After the almost obligatory period of bitterness, blame and animosity we assumed a kind of truce and to be quite honest, I'd now consider her a friend again. I even went to the wedding when she got married again!

Does this sound like a recurring theme?

Then, about five years ago, through a very strange set of circumstances, I fell for a girl who was a lot younger than me but who was very much on the same wavelength. We had a roller coaster ride of a relationship for a few years but it ended in tears and not without a fair amount of pain on both sides. I could write volumes about our time together but I guess it's best kept private. There are two sides to every argument!

Finally, I had an 'almost but not quite' liaison with someone I've grown to care for a lot over the past year or so. She was there for me when I badly needed a friend and we've become very close. We could become closer, but she's with someone to whom she keeps giving a 'last chance'. I'll wait, but not forever.

Anyway, I suppose that's a fair and honest assessment of my most notable romantic involvements. I wouldn't have liked to have missed out on any of them, or indeed several others who I haven't mentioned, but the end result is that I'm still looking for that 'dream girl'. Maybe I've always been looking too hard, maybe I've been too selective. Who knows how things are going to work out. All I know is that I've never deliberately hurt them and upon reflection I could have been happy with any of them. Maybe.

So, here I am again. Starting over, moving house, moving on. A bit older, a bit wiser (perhaps!) but still the same, soppy, idealistic dreamer that I was all those years ago. I wouldn't ever like to change my attitude toward romance, or towards life in general. I think I'm OK and those that matter think I'm OK too. That'll do for me.

WHEN SPRING COMES
Doreen Cawley

At last summer was over and the holidaymakers had left, peace and tranquillity had descended upon our sleepy little village. It lay in a small vale surrounded by hills covered in heather. The colours were now changing to gold and orange giving you a sense that autumn would soon be upon us, it was a spectacular sight to see as the hills were ablaze with colour.

It had been a wonderful summer, so many visitors and holidaymakers who brought wealth and work to the village, but it was nice to get it back to some normality and seeing some familiar faces which seemed to be missing during the summer. The cobbled streets and whitewashed cottages were a main attraction. The small shops were filled with craftwork made by the locals and many of their crafts were handed down from generations. I knew this summer had been special, meeting David had changed my life and a little sadness swept over me at the passing of summer.

My favourite pastime was browsing around the art shops in Moreton, most of the paintings were done by local artists. I admired their skills, the watercolours blending together as if the paintings were real. Although the art shops were rather small and dreary, the hanging artwork could distract you from the peeling paint and age-stained walls. It was during one of these days while walking around admiring the pictures that one of them caught my eye. Trying to look at it from every angle I bumped into someone. 'Sorry,' I said. As I turned around I found myself looking into the bluest eyes I had ever seen. I was concentrating on the picture.

He smiled and said, 'That's OK.'

'Do you like the painting?' I said.

'It's not bad, but it could be better,' he said, turning back to look at it.

I felt annoyed at his criticism of the local artists who I knew and liked. I decided to question him further but this proved difficult. I said I thought it was rather good, but then I am no expert. I waited for a response but none was forthcoming. 'Are you an artist?'

'No,' he replied, turning to face me again.

'But you know something about it?' I said.

'I know what I like,' he retorted.

I asked him what he did for a living and he replied that he taught art in the school where he lived.

'Where is that?' I asked.

'In a small town called Cottingham, about 90 miles from here.' He told me his name was David and I introduced myself as Wendy and that I had lived in Moreton all my life.

Although he was beginning to irritate me, I felt drawn to him even though he had an annoying air of arrogance about him. 'Do you often visit the art shops around here?' I asked.

'Fairly often, mostly on my own,' he replied. He then turned and walked away.

I decided not to pursue this conversation for the moment, so I walked out of the shop.

The next day I decided to go to the beach and do some sunbathing and swimming, the sun was out and there was not a cloud in the sky. As I walked down to the sea I heard someone call my name. I turned round and there was David.

'Sorry about yesterday,' he said, 'can we start again?'

I looked at him. 'Why not? I have nothing better to do.'

'Neither have I,' he said. He asked me what I did for a living.

'I work in the local solicitor's office, I have been there since leaving school.'

'Do you have any ambitions?' he asked.

'Not really. Eventually I would like to get married and have a family. Do you have any ambitions?' I asked.

He turned to look at me and said, 'A full-time artist and to own my own art shop, somewhere I could sell my paintings.'

'What other things do you enjoy?' I asked.

'Walking, climbing, I go away most weekends with my friends doing outdoor activities.'

Evidently he had a hectic lifestyle, but I knew I wanted to get to know him better.

David and I would walk along the beach listening to the waves lapping the shore. We would take our shoes off and paddle in the sea. There were sailing boats bobbing up and down, the wind would catch their sails and blow them further out to sea. Each evening we would go down to the harbour and watch the small fishing boats bringing in their daily catch and the seagulls hovering overhead could smell the fish, hoping for an easy supper. These were wonderful moments but I knew they would eventually come to an end. David would go back to his world and I would stay here in Moreton.

Before David's holiday was over, he asked me if I would let him paint a portrait of me, something for him to remember me by, and the wonderful holiday we had shared together. Each day we would go down to the beach, David would set his easel up and start painting. I enjoyed these days sitting for David, not wanting them to end, but all too soon the portrait was finished. When David unveiled it I could not believe it was me, I looked quite beautiful.

I knew the time had come when we would have to part. We said our goodbyes and David promised he would be back in the spring, as autumn and winter were a busy time of the year at school with the outdoor activities. Winter came and the days seemed dark and dismal, and summer was just a memory. Christmas arrived, but there was no word from David. Had he forgotten about me? I kept myself busy, hoping it would stop me thinking about David, but to no avail. Memories of our time together would come flooding back and I knew I must get my life back, so I started going out with my friends.

Spring came with anticipation, gardens filled with daffodils, blossom breaking out on the trees; it was a lovely time of the year with everything coming to life. I walked along the beach thinking of David, when I noticed someone walking towards me. As we got closer I realised it was David and that he had kept his promise. I ran towards him, his arms were open wide and all I could think about was that he was here and so was spring.

THE FINAL AFFAIR
Susie Field

Anne stared at the bulging suitcases resting on her bed, her mind racing. How could he let her down again? He'd promised. They were just empty words. Wiping away the tears, she slowly walked down the stairs and into the sitting room. It was a beautiful room, exquisitely furnished over the years with love and care.

'Are you OK, Mum?' Sandy asked, poking his head round the door. 'I was just going out. You look awful.'

Anne smiled at her handsome son - the mirror image of Marcus. Only the week before, they'd celebrated Sandy's eighteenth birthday. It had been a wonderful party surrounded by family and friends. She'd been so happy with Marcus by her side, the perfect couple. It had all been a lie.

'I have the beginnings of a headache, love,' Anne replied, forcing another smile.

'Can I get you anything?' Sandy asked with concern.

Anne shook her head. 'No, it's all right love. I'll have a lie down. Don't you worry.'

Sandy bent to kiss her cheek and then he was gone. Anne poured herself a strong Martini and waited.

'I'm home, darling,' Marcus shouted from the hall before striding into the sitting room. At forty-one years old he was a handsome man, tall with thick blond hair. He was in good shape, thanks to twice weekly visits to the gym. This wasn't his first affair, but Anne knew it would be his last. He'd promised five years ago that he would never stray again. How he had cried and begged for forgiveness, said how much he loved her and she loved him - still did, but enough was enough. It was time to move on.

'Is anything wrong?' he asked.

Anne stared at him coldly. Marcus swallowed, he recognised that look.

'How could you?' she said quietly. 'How could you do this to me Marcus?'

'How could I do what?' he replied, his heart thumping in his chest.

'Don't insult me Marcus by trying to deny it,' Anne snapped. 'I trusted you. What a fool I've been.'

'Please Anne, I can explain,' Marcus grabbed her hand.

'Don't bother,' Anne replied, pulling away from him. 'With my own sister. Betrayed by the two people I love most in the world. Why Marcus?'

'I don't know,' he replied, not meeting her gaze. 'I was weak. She came on to me, I should have said no. It's over, I swear.'

'No, it's not over,' Anne yelled. 'She's pregnant.'

'Pregnant,' Marcus mouthed. This was a disaster.

'Have you any idea how that makes me feel? My younger sister phoned to tell me she is pregnant with my husband's baby.'

'I didn't know. What's she going to do?' he said almost to himself.

'How the hell do I know?' Anne yelled. 'I didn't ask. I was too shocked, stunned by the enormity of such a betrayal.'

'I'm sorry,' Marcus said quietly. 'I never expected this to happen.'

'It's what happens when two people have unprotected sex,' Anne shouted.

Marcus ran his fingers though his hair and buried his face in his hands. 'Is she sure it's mine?' he asked.

'She says it is,' Anne replied.

'I'm not the only one she's been sleeping with. I'll demand tests.'

'Don't bother on my account,' Anne sighed. She was suddenly desperately tired. 'I don't care. I want you to leave now.'

'Leave,' Marcus gasped. 'Where am I supposed to go?'

'I'm sure Suzanne would be more than happy to give you a bed for the night,' Anne replied angrily.

She would calm down, Marcus told himself. She was furious, but she would calm down. Suzanne wouldn't want kids at 35, she was a career woman through and through. She'd opt for an abortion. Anne needed some space, that was all. 'OK,' he said at last. 'I'll pack a few things.' God this was awful.

'Your things are already packed,' Anne said calmly. 'Just get out.'

'What about the kids? They'll want to know where I am.'

'Tell them the truth,' Anne replied sadly. 'That'll be a first for you I'm sure.'

'They'll be upset,' Marcus said, playing for time.

'You should have thought of that,' Anne said.

'I'll let you know where I'm staying,' Marcus replied. 'I won't be at Suzanne's, like I said, it's over.'

'I don't believe it,' Sandy gasped. 'It's disgusting. With Auntie Suzanne of all people. How could they do this to us Mum?'

Anne shook her head. Sandy was livid.

'Has Daddy gone forever?' Laura sobbed.

'Of course not sweetheart,' Anne replied, pulling Laura into her arms. 'He's still your father, that won't change. You can see him whenever you want.'

'Well I don't want to see him,' Sandy snapped. 'He can go to Hell for all I care.'

'Sandy, please,' Anne begged. 'Laura's upset. Let's not make things worse.'

'They couldn't be any worse,' Sandy replied. 'What are you going to do, Mum?'

'I'm filing for a divorce,' Anne replied.

'Will we have to move?' Laura asked through her tears. At sixteen years old, she was a daddy's girl. She loved her home and her parents. The devastation showed clearly on her pretty face.

'I'm not sure love, maybe,' Anne answered truthfully. 'But not for a while. Daddy will always support you, don't worry.'

'I can support myself thanks,' Sandy stated vehemently. 'I won't bother going to uni.'

'Yes you will Sandy,' Anne insisted. 'Your father and I will sort things out financially. I can always work extra hours at the estate agents. Now off you go and get ready for bed Laura. I'll be up in a moment.

'There's something else you should know Sandy,' Anne was dreading telling him. 'I didn't want to say anything in front of Laura. Auntie Suzanne's pregnant.'

'My God,' Sandy slumped back onto the settee. 'This gets worse and worse.'

Anne could no longer hold back the tears. She hadn't wanted to cry in front of Sandy, but her heart was breaking. 'I loved him so much, Sandy,' she sobbed.

'I know Mum,' Sandy replied, putting a comforting arm around her shoulders. 'We'll be OK, you'll see.'

'Yes we will,' Anne replied with a sudden determination she didn't feel.

'You look as though you could do with a coffee?' Marcus glanced up at his secretary.'

'Thanks,' he said. 'I wish a coffee would solve my problems.'

'Things no better then?' Megan asked, taking a chair.

Marcus shook his head. 'How did I make such a mess of things Megan?'

'I don't think you need me to tell you that,' she smiled. Megan was a good looking woman in her late thirties. She'd been Marcus' secretary for ten years and at first Marcus had flirted outrageously with her, but she'd made it clear, she was happily married and their relationship was strictly business. Since that moment they'd become friends as well as colleagues.

'I know, I know,' Marcus sighed. 'I've only myself to blame. I still love Anne, I just didn't realise how much. I felt sure I'd be able to talk her round in time, but it's been five months. She's filed for divorce, put the house up for sale. I loved that house.'

'How's Suzanne?' Megan asked. She couldn't help feeling sorry for Marcus.

'Fat,' he replied simply.

'Do you love her?' Megan asked.

'No I don't,' Marcus replied sadly. 'I'm only staying because of the baby. I'm not even sure it's mine. I wasn't the only guy she was seeing.'

'Messy,' Megan answered, wrinkling her nose. 'How's Laura and Sandy?'

'Laura seems OK. As for Sandy, every time he looks at me - pure hatred. You wouldn't believe it.'

'Protective of his mother I suppose,' Megan said thoughtfully.

'I'm sure you're right. He's at uni most of the time, only home for the holidays, which reminds me, I'm taking them out for a meal tonight. Can't say I'm looking forward to seeing Sandy - that's if he even bothers to turn up.'

'I'm sorry Marcus,' Megan said, taking his hand, 'I really am.'

'So am I,' he whispered. 'So am I.'

'Can I have a pudding, Daddy?' Laura asked sweetly, smiling at her father.

'Yes of course,' Marcus replied, signalling the waitress. 'What about you Sandy?'

'No thanks,' Sandy replied solemnly. 'I've had enough.'

Laura excused herself to go to the ladies room, leaving Marcus and Sandy alone. An uncomfortable silence followed.

'How's your mum?' Marcus asked eventually.

'Do you care?' Sandy replied.

'Of course I do,' Marcus snapped.

'She's fine,' Sandy answered. 'Looks great. She's lost weight and she's working full-time at the estate agents. I think her boss fancies her.'

'Frank Beaumont,' Marcus replied. 'I wouldn't have thought he was Anne's type.'

'They're dating,' Sandy added rather smugly. It wasn't entirely true. They'd only been out for lunch a couple of times, but he loved seeing his father squirm. Served him right.

'Are you sure?' Marcus asked. He'd never liked Frank Beaumont, as far as he was concerned, he was a creep. What a nerve making a move on Anne when she was so vulnerable.

'Certain,' Sandy said, meeting his father's eye. 'By the way, Mum's got a buyer for the house.'

'Really,' Marcus remarked, feeling sick inside. Things were moving too quickly.

'Yep,' Sandy continued, 'Mum's put a deposit on one of those new apartments. She can't wait to move out, a fresh start she said.'

Laura returned to the table and the conversation ended abruptly.

'I was thinking,' Marcus said turning to Laura, 'I thought we'd take a holiday, just the three of us.'

'What about Auntie Suzanne and the baby?' Sandy asked with a hint of sarcasm.

'I meant in a few months' time,' Marcus continued. 'Perhaps early next year, possibly around Easter time. What do you say guys?'

'Count me out,' Sandy replied. 'I've got things planned.'

Marcus nodded. No surprise there.

'I'll come,' Laura said eagerly. 'Can I bring a friend?'

'Of course,' Marcus said, taking her hand.

'Marcus, what a surprise,' Anne said on hearing his voice. She hadn't expected this particular phone call.

'How are you?' Marcus asked, amazed at how calm he sounded.

'I'm fine,' she replied. 'And you?'

'OK,' he answered. 'Sandy said you had a buyer for the house?'

'It's not definite,' Anne replied. Trust Sandy to gloat. 'But I'm very hopeful.'

'That's good,' Marcus answered. It was anything but good. 'I thought we should meet, you know, to discuss the implications of the house sale. I want things to be amicable for the sake of the kids.'

'Of course,' Anne answered.

'I thought perhaps dinner - tomorrow night?' Marcus asked casually.

'I don't think that's a good idea,' Anne answered.

'Why not?' Marcus continued. 'I'll book a table at Prego's, you love it there.'

'OK,' Anne said eventually. 'I suppose we do have a lot to discuss. What about Suzanne, won't she mind?'

'Of course not,' Marcus lied - she'd be livid, but he had no intention of telling her. 'Shall I pick you up - say 7.30?'

'No, I'll meet you there,' Anne said, replacing the receiver.

'Yes!' Marcus yelled. His plan had worked. One last try, Anne was worth it. Superb Italian food, plenty of wine. He knew Anne still loved him, who knows what might happen?

Marcus stood as Anne approached. She looked fantastic as she moved towards him. She had lost weight - yet in all the right places. The green crepe dress hugged her full breasts and slim hips. Several heads turned as she headed his way.

'You look wonderful,' Marcus said, kissing her cheek.

'So do you,' Anne replied, and he did. He looked immaculate in a soft grey cashmere suit - his hair carefully groomed. He was a handsome man, no wonder women loved him. The conversation flowed easily throughout the meal, the food was good and Anne felt slightly heady - too much wine.

'No more for me,' she said as Marcus reached for the bottle. 'I've had enough.'

Marcus ordered coffee and they chatted about the kids, and eventually the conversation turned to the pending house sale. 'It'll be a shame to see the house go,' Marcus said slowly, his eyes never leaving Anne's face. 'I loved that house. So many memories.'

'Not always good ones,' Anne whispered.

'Come on Anne,' he said, taking her hand. She did not pull away. 'We've had some good times, wonderful times. I wish we could turn back the clock.'

'It's too late, Marcus,' Anne said quietly, feeling the warmth of his fingers as they caressed her palm. 'It's time to move on. I hope we can be friends.'

'I don't like the sound of friends,' Marcus replied.

'Friendship is all I can give you now Marcus.'

'If you say so,' he replied. Their eyes met and held. Anne quickly looked away and Marcus signalled for the bill.

'Thanks for a lovely meal,' Anne said as Marcus walked her to the door. He hated to see the 'For Sale' sign looming menacingly in the garden. It still felt like home to Marcus. Suzanne's flat didn't have the same appeal. It was Anne he wanted.

'Don't I get a coffee?' Marcus asked, giving Anne the benefit of his charming smile.

'That's not a good idea,' Anne said with some hesitation.

'Oh come on,' Marcus grinned, 'don't you trust me?'

'Actually no, I don't,' Anne replied truthfully, yet she still allowed Marcus to follow her inside. It was a mistake. As soon as she closed the door, Marcus pulled her into his arms and kissed her gently. When she didn't resist, he deepened the kiss, to which she responded. It felt so good to be in his arms again. She could feel his desire as his hands caressed her body.

'Oh Anne, Anne,' he breathed, 'I've never stopped loving you. It was always you.'

'Marcus, I don't think this is a good idea …' she began, but he swept her into his arms and carried her upstairs.

Anne woke with a start, her head was pounding. She turned to see Marcus - his handsome face so innocent in sleep.

'Hi,' he said, suddenly opening his eyes.

Slowly the memory of the previous evening returned to Anne. Thank goodness Sandy was at uni, he would be disgusted at her weakness.

'You'd better go before Laura wakes,' Anne said, pulling the duvet around her naked body.

'Why?' Marcus asked. 'She'll have to know sooner or later. She'll be thrilled when I move back in.'

'What are you talking about?' Anne asked. 'We're getting a divorce, the house is as good as sold.'

'It's not too late to pull out,' Marcus continued.

'I don't want to pull out Marcus. Nothing's changed.'

'But I thought after last night, well you know, we made love, it was good, wasn't it?'

'We had sex Marcus,' Anne said firmly, 'that's all.'

'You mean it meant nothing,' Marcus felt a surge of panic.

'Let's get one thing straight,' Anne answered. 'Last night was good, I admit it. I wanted sex, you were available and happen to be quite good at it, and yes, I did enjoy it, but now I'd like you to leave.'

'You're throwing me out?' Marcus couldn't believe this was happening.

'I'm asking you to leave,' Anne responded quietly.

A silence fell between them, broken suddenly by the shrill ringing of the telephone.

'Hello,' Anne said sharply.

It was Suzanne. 'Is Marcus there?' she was almost hysterical.

'Yes, he's here,' Anne replied.

'I knew it,' Suzanne was sobbing uncontrollably, and in spite of herself, Anne felt sympathy for her sister, she knew how it felt.

'The lying, cheating bastard,' Suzanne yelled into the phone.

'I won't disagree,' Anne said, somewhat smugly.

'Tell him to go to Hell,' Suzanne screamed. 'And tell him it's not even his baby.'

'Tell him yourself,' Anne replied, passing the telephone to Marcus.

Climbing out of bed, she headed for the shower. When she returned to the bedroom, he was gone.

'Good morning,' Frank said as Anne walked into the office. 'Did you enjoy your week off?'

'Yes thank you,' Anne replied, flashing him a smile. He was such an attractive man. Why hadn't she ever noticed?

'Did you get everything sorted out?' Frank asked with concern.

'Yes I did,' Anne replied, looking directly at him. 'Well and truly sorted.'

WHAT A WEEK!
Janice Melmoth

'Who's got a big birthday coming up?' This repetitive question was all I had heard lately. Closely followed by, 'Are you having a party and how are you going to celebrate this momentous occasion?'

I did not want a party. I did not want my picture in the paper. In fact I just wanted the forthcoming event to slip quietly by. After considerable thought I came up with an idea which, as it evolved, became quite exciting.

I wanted to see my family and friends, but I wanted quality time with them. I wanted to remember what we talked about and dress in different outfits, in fact I wanted my birthday to last the whole week and nothing less than the whole week ... and that was my birthday plan.

Having explained this to my family and friends, my trademark diary started to fill.

On Friday the 8th October, bags and clothes on hangers adorned by car. I made my way over to my daughter's house. My car groaned with yet another suitcase and clothes on hangers. We headed for the motorway with the sun shining and the thought of our 'leisure break' weekend.

Arriving at reception, we collected our key to room 302, where we quickly unpacked, then headed for the heated pool and steam room; thoughts of our meal on table 152 and the evening entertainment sounded promising.

The following day we had our pre-booked massage, manicure, pedicure and facial. It was heaven. Sunday, being the *big* day, my daughter had secretly arranged room service of champagne, flowers, chocolate and fruit, the entire weekend was superb ...

On Tuesday 12th, I was swimming at my local leisure club contemplating the day ahead. I was meeting a friend at noon who I used to work with, so I was looking forward to catching up. Lunch was enjoyed in a small town which boasts a lovely harbour.

In the evening, I met three girlfriends who I also used to work with, we had arranged bowling and a pub meal. Well, that was worth a box of tissues. None of us could bowl and two of us nearly set the alarms off. The conversation was invigorating, diverse, private and personal. Very good friends who I see every four to five weeks.

Wednesday 13th was a lunch time meeting with a friend who had climbed halfway up Ben Nevis with me, we talked avidly about our forthcoming 'Yorkshire Three Peak Challenge' and the extra walking we needed to do to make sure we completed the 26 miles.

Driving home I was acutely aware of the time I had to shower, change my clothes then head for the Mexican restaurant. The two 'girls' that I was to share the evening with I had met in March 1990, when we began our nurse training. We have kept in touch and met regularly, so you can imagine the history between us.

As I drove home later, I reflected on my evening and realised that I had some very special friends.

Thursday lunch time was taken care of, my car was booked in for a service! So I had time to think about the evening. I was going to a Greek restaurant with three friends from work, where I enjoyed the Tava Horiatikos, a spicy pork dish, followed by bayota dessert! I tend to decline dessert for obvious reasons! The evenings we spent together always ran out of time before our lively conversations ended. I was so glad a policeman didn't stop me on the way home and ask why I was smiling … you cannot explain friendship.

Friday 15th dawned bright and early with another swim and a visit from a very nice man who came to service my central heating system. I met him over two years ago when we both started a college course, so over coffee and croissants we caught up …

Friday evening looked promising. A friend was coming to stay over, as we planned a night in town. This time the venue for the meal was a bistro. 'Does my bum look big in these?' 'This top or that one?' The usual questions as we hurtled up and down the stairs, drinking wine and answering our mobiles. I felt sure we would be late for our table booking.

Thankfully we arrived on time, comfortable in each other's company and looking forward to the evening ahead. After a splendid meal of chicken fajitas and oodles of peppers, washed down by a very nice white wine, we went for drinks in town before going to a well known nightclub. I had not been there for two years and can only describe it as an eye-opener. We were chatted to, chatted up and chatted over. The best chat-up line had to go to a very young, questionable 18-year-old. 'Do you want to dance, or are you married?'

On the way home we laughed and both felt we had gained an insight into night clubbing! When we arrived home, our conversation continued over another bottle of wine, we were also keeping one eye on the clock. My friend now only had two hours left before getting ready to go to work and I had only three before embarking on a day's coastal walking!

I think I fared a little better as I strolled up steep hills with my walking friend of 11 years, stopping every now and then to look at our beautiful countryside and drinking water which tasted like nectar. It was good to catch up.

I stayed in Saturday night. Yes, I can hear you say, 'It's Saturday night,' but I was tired, I had been out every night!

I woke up Sunday morning completely refreshed and looking forward to a traditional roast dinner with my family. I had enjoyed a splendid week and this was the icing on the cake.

As the day closed in, I recaptured the events of the past week. I have some very special friends and thoroughly enjoyed meeting them all and spending quality time together. I received some beautiful presents and lovely cards, but most of all I want to say thank you to each and every one of them for sharing my 50th birthday in such a special way.

A treasured memory ...

AT RAINBOW'S END
Christina B Cox

Driving steadily down the rutted muddy track, the fading watery sun slowly disappearing into gathering cloud and descending darkness. Claire's hands cradled her protruding belly feeling every judder and bump. Lambs and rabbits scampered in the adjacent fields, and crows and woodpigeon flew among the trees. Rainbow's End, the idyllic cottage, sat in its perfect setting, surrounded by endless green fields speckled with woodlands. Smoke rose high into the air from the tall chimneys. Ivy clung to its ancient walls and roses rambled haphazardly amongst the green leaves.

Mrs Cooper the caretaker met them at the door and led them both inside. In the warm cosy living room a roaring log fire crackled its greeting in the inglenook fireplace, the smell of burning logs wafted around the room.

'Sit yourselves down my dears,' said the kindly old caretaker, 'the kettle's just boiling.'

'When is it due?' she questioned Claire, watching as she struggled to lever herself into the comfy cottage chair.

'Oh, about six weeks time,' she answered, 'we can't wait, we're so looking forward to having a baby around.'

'It will be a busy time for you both but wonderful none the less.' Her words coming from years of experience.

The welcome pot of tea appeared in no time. Mrs Cooper sat and chatted whilst handing round the plate of biscuits.

Claire and Matt waved off Mrs Cooper after exploring the remainder of the house.

'I love it here,' Claire said to Matt.

'Yes it does have a certain charm about it,' he agreed. 'You will definitely be able to get the rest that your doctor ordered,' he fussed. They busied themselves settling in and unpacking food and clothing.

Mrs Cooper had left them milk and a hamper in the kitchen with immediate essentials. After soup and sandwiches they retired to bed.

Claire snuggled down under the duvet, and fondled her belly Matt sound asleep beside her. Smiling inwardly to herself she thought, *very soon we shall be parents,* but couldn't help thinking of all the miscarriages she had had over the years, both had almost given up on the thought that they would ever have a baby of their own. But this time

Claire had managed to keep the baby, they were over the moon with joy.

The April sun streamed into the bedroom. 'What a beautiful day,' said Claire as Matt came through the door with a breakfast tray. 'You're spoiling me,' smiled Claire.

Matt kissed her forehead tenderly, 'Well you're *both* worth it.'

The morning was spent exploring the village nearby. Inquisitive eyes followed them as they wandered through the streets. It was a village where everyone knew everyone and suddenly they were the strangers in their midst. One or two bade them 'Good morning' and seemed friendly, though one elderly lady walking with a stick, face turned white when she eyed Claire as though she had seen a ghost.

They next visited the local church which seemed to invite them in, and pondered on the weather-beaten gravestones dotted around the churchyard.

'We really ought to get you home to put your feet up, remember what the doctor said.'

'Yes OK coming,' taking a last look at the grave of a young girl.

Claire was awoken one night by the sound of a baby crying. Eyes wide open she listened intently and couldn't believe her ears. Matt, fast asleep oblivious to all. She didn't try to wake him, it was almost as if she was too selfish to share this moment. Reaching for her dressing gown she made her way towards the attic room. The dim light still worked and emphasised the creaky old wooden staircase leading to a door at the top. A faint light flickered beneath it. The crying got louder as she climbed the stairs and was now joined by the sobbing of a woman. Her hand reached gingerly towards the door. She gently pushed it open inch by inch. There stood a young woman in a long flowing night-gown holding a tiny baby in her arms, the woman no more than a teenager. Their eyes met fleetingly, a face racked by sadness, flowing dark hair hanging limply on her shoulders.

In an instant breeze the figure disappeared leaving only the lighted candles last flicker and the cradle swinging to and fro, echoing the silence. It was as if they never were. Claire stood for a while just gazing into the empty room, feeling the lingering chill, but somehow she was not afraid.

In the morning Claire questioned Matt. As she thought, he had heard nothing. She now began to wonder if she had dreamed it. She'd tried the attic door, it was locked. Matt looked at her oddly and for once she knew he did not believe the story she told him. He took himself off for a walk.

Claire was not convinced. When Mrs Cooper arrived she cornered her in the kitchen and asked who had lived in this house before and if any young girl had lived in the attic with a baby.

'What have you heard?' she asked warily stepping backwards. 'You get strange noises in the countryside you know, noises which sound like other things.'

'I know what I heard Mrs Cooper and I know what I saw.' Feeling more convinced than ever now it was not a dream.

'Seen, what have you seen?' Realising too late she had said too much. 'Dear God, she's not back is she?' Mrs Cooper looked straight into Claire's eyes. 'You had better sit yourself down my dear and I'll tell you what I know.'

Mrs Cooper started her story which began some seventy, eighty or more years ago. 'A farming family lived in Rainbow's End making a good living from the farm. They had five children, three boys and two girls, and were well respected in the village. One day the eldest girl, then sixteen managed to get herself pregnant with a young boy from the village, nothing was said to the villagers - well in those days attitudes were somewhat different,' she added. 'As soon as the girl started to show, it was said she had gone to help her aunt who was ill, but in fact she had been sent up to the attic to live her life, cruel if you ask me.'

Claire listened intently.

'She was never allowed to see the light of day, only from her window, so there she spent each day. Soon after her baby was born it was taken from her, and she never saw it again. Some say it was given to a family out of town. Each night her crying was put down to the whistling wind. Her young man was sent to join the army in disgrace, sadly he was killed in some battle or other. Somehow the girl found out and she was never the same again. Choosing to live in the attic she soon died of a broken heart. She's buried in the village churchyard you know.'

'What was her name Mrs Cooper?' Claire enquired.

'Vicky, no Victoria Goodman if my memory serves me right.'

'I was looking at her gravestone only last week, how strange.'

'Her sister, she's nearly ninety now, lives in the village, she and the family moved from here when night after night Vicky's crying was heard even after she was dead and buried.'

'What happened to the child?' Claire continued with her questions.

'As I said some say it went to a family out of town but I've heard other stories of how the child was badly treated and died very young.'

'It's such a sad story Mrs Cooper, how could people be so cruel?'

'It was different in those days my dear, I'm not saying its right mind.'

'I'm wonderin' if the fact that you are pregnant has disturbed her again,' Mrs Cooper pondered.

'Perhaps you shouldn't stay here my dear, maybe you should leave soon.'

'I'm not afraid Mrs Cooper, I think she's appeared to me for a reason, I'm going to find out why.'

'Well if you are quite sure my dear you in your tender state.'

'Quite sure Mrs Cooper.'

Mrs Cooper got the attic key, then together they made their way to the attic door so that Claire could see the room in daylight. The room was sparse, no carpet, only stained floorboards. A single bed in one corner, a dressing table, chair, and the baby crib. Cobwebs hung in drapes, the windows unwashed, curtains threadbare. 'I really must give this room a clean,' said Mrs Cooper. Claire seemed not to hear but instead stared into the empty crib.

Claire having told Matt Mrs Cooper's story again made their way to the churchyard to view Victoria Goodman's gravestone, she was nineteen years old when she died needlessly.

A lone rose had been placed on the grave, maybe her younger sister.

Each night the crying was heard, and each night Claire climbed the stairs to the attic. The baby was now nowhere to be seen, just Victoria staring into the empty swinging crib. As before she disappeared when she saw Claire, leaving the same cold chill in the night air.

Matt slept through all of it till one night Claire woke him. Startled, he accompanied Claire up the attic stairs. Victoria vanished in a wispy haze. But Matt had seen her too.

'We should leave,' he said.

'No,' said Claire. 'She means us no harm.'

A few hours later Claire's labour started much earlier than intended. Mrs Cooper called an ambulance and Claire was whisked off to hospital. Matt stayed in a hotel in town not wanting to spend the night at the cottage.

A beautiful baby girl was delivered to her the next day. A normal delivery and a perfect baby. 'We think you may have got your dates wrong Mrs Sheldon,' the doctor told Claire. 'She seems like a full term baby, you can go home in a day or two.'

Matt and Claire were ecstatic about their new baby daughter. 'I would like to call her Victoria,' Claire told Matt.

'It's as good as any name I suppose,' so it was agreed.

Mrs Cooper was there to greet them when they all arrived home from hospital. She came with armfuls of baby clothes and bedding. 'I know you didn't bring any baby things with you so the villagers have helped out.'

'That's so kind,' said Claire.

'You could use the old crib in the attic for a day or two, I've cleaned it up and aired it well.'

'No,' said Matt angrily.

'I think it would be a great idea Mrs Cooper, thank you,' Claire interrupted.

Claire placed the baby in the crib in the warm sitting room, and she slept soundly. And in the evening carried the baby and crib into the bedroom.

Claire was roused from her sleep not by her crying baby but by a chill that entered the room. Victoria Goodman was standing over the crib admiring the new baby girl. Her face was no longer streaked with tears but a smile spread across her lips, she seemed happy now and content, and then she was gone.

Mrs Cooper fussed around Claire and the baby like a broody hen till in a peaceful moment when the baby was asleep she looked at Claire and said, 'I never did tell you how much you look like Victoria Goodman. I've seen her photos, it's quite uncanny really.'

'She's at peace now Mrs Cooper,' Claire said, 'she hasn't been back the last few nights.'

'Well that's good,' remarked Mrs Cooper. 'I was talking to her sister in the village the other day, you gave her a rare shock it seems when she saw you in the village.'

'Oh that will be the old lady we saw,' Claire suddenly realised.

Matt and Claire left Rainbow's End a few days later, the sun shone but rain also threatened and just for a moment a rainbow appeared in the sky above the cottage. They came back year after year with their daughter Victoria.

But one day they knew that Victoria would make Rainbow's End her home.

A CHANCE ENCOUNTER
Margaret Ward

As I walked through the park I saw her again, she was sitting on the same bench all alone. The park was a short cut used by many to reach the town, thus avoiding the busy streets congested with cars. I walk through it twice a day to reach my workplace, as a receptionist at a hotel and then home again. Three times this week she had been there. She didn't seem much older than I was, although I knew that looks could be deceptive. I started wondering what thoughts went through her mind as she sat so still on the bench, and why a park bench was more favourable than a comfortable chair. Maybe she was homeless, she was young and pretty and seemed to enjoy the solitude of the park before going about her day.

I hadn't lived in this area for long; it was still relatively new to me. I had moved down to Devon from Yorkshire to make a fresh start after a broken relationship. My parents lived in Yorkshire; they had adopted me as a baby after realising that they couldn't have any children of their own. My birth mother had been very young and had no partner, so gave me up for adoption.

On arriving in Devon I found myself a flat and a job as a receptionist in a nearby hotel. It was hard at first but was settling in and life was getting better.

My thoughts kept returning to the woman on the park bench as I went about my work during the day. Why I didn't know, but somehow I knew in my mind that I had to find out more about her. I decided that the following morning I would leave for work earlier, then if she was in the park I could stop and say hello. I didn't know why I was interested in her, I knew that she might tell me to go away in no uncertain terms, but I felt that I had to take that chance.

It had been extremely busy in the hotel and I wasn't sorry to head for home. Walking through my front door peace and calm enveloped me. This was my own space and I loved it. During the evening my thoughts once again returned to the woman in the park, and after a phone call to my parents I turned in for the night and drifted off into a restless sleep.

The next morning as I made my way through the park earlier than normal, I spotted her on the same bench. I made my way to the bench but instead of walking past it, as I had done many times before, I sat down beside her. I took a sideways glance at her and noticed that she looked my age which was thirty. Her hair was shoulder length and dyed a blonde colour, she didn't wear make-up and looked very dishevelled.

'Hello,' I said. There was no reply. She was looking straight ahead of her and seemed completely oblivious of me being there. 'It's a lovely morning isn't it,' I proceeded to try and make conversation but still no response. Oh well at least I had tried, that's all I could have done really, clearly she wanted to be left alone and I could respect that. I got up from the bench and started walking away, suddenly I felt someone pulling on my sleeve, turning around sharply I saw her standing beside me. She was using sign language to tell me something, but I didn't understand anything like this so I just shrugged my shoulders.

What I did understand though was that this was clearly the reason that she had ignored me on the bench for she was deaf. There I was assuming that she wanted to be left alone, this I realised was my first lesson in learning to never assume. She opened her palm out and indicated with her other hand that she wanted to write something down. I found some paper and a pen in my bag and passed them to her. After a little while she gave it back to me, she had written that her name was Stephanie, that she was deaf and homeless, and I have been very kind to take the trouble to try and talk to her. I responded by writing down that I would meet her in the morning, and as it was Sunday would be able to spend more time with her, as I didn't have to go to work. She put my note into her pocket, smiled at me and walked away. Whether she would be there the following day remained to be seen.

Stephanie had intrigued me for reasons that I didn't understand, now realising that she was deaf I felt that I wanted to try and do something to help her. How I didn't know, but I would think about that if and when the time came.

The next morning Stephanie was waiting for me, as I approached her she smiled at me. It was a lovely sunny morning and the sun beamed down on us as we sat together on the bench. I had taken a pad and pen with me so we could communicate, looking at Stephanie I knew that she hadn't enjoyed the pleasure of bathing for a while. The jeans she was wearing were threadbare and her jumper was too large, her hair needed washing and her shoes were worn down. I felt sorry for her looking in such a bad way but maybe she liked being like this, it wasn't for me to comment on. I gave Stephanie my paper and pen and she proceeded to write, after about thirty minutes she passed the piece of paper back to me. As I read what she had written, I could feel her eyes on me waiting for my reaction. This is what she had written ...

'My name is Stephanie Lawrence, my mother was only fifteen when she gave birth to me, she had no partner so put me up for adoption. It was a job to find me parents because of my handicap of being deaf, but adoptive parents were found and they loved me dearly, but when I was eight they were both killed in a car accident, no other family members were prepared to take me on so I was placed in a children's home. It wasn't nice in the home and I had no family to visit me. When I was sixteen I ran away from there and tried to start afresh but it was very difficult. I went to London and lived on the streets with others that I had made friends with. I have met nasty and nice people, I am now thirty-two and because of my handicap many people assume that I am stupid. I was born up north and went to London just over a year ago. I have been in Devon for about 4 months now for a change of scenery and to try my luck here. It's very quiet down here so unlike London, I have nowhere to stay as no one will take me seriously or give me a job. That's until you took the trouble to sit beside me on this bench, you are very kind'.

As I read the scenario of her life tears welled up in my eyes. I always thought that my life had started badly but at least my adoptive parents were still with me and loved me very much. I could have so easily found myself in Stephanie's position. I felt Stephanie looking intensely at me wondering what my reaction would be. I was thirty, she was thirty-two, when I first saw her I had felt she was near my age. I turned towards her and slid my arm around her shoulders, I then took hold of my pen and replied to her saying that I was thirty years old, came from Yorkshire and had recently moved to Devon after a split from my boyfriend. I too had been adopted by a lovely couple that I had always considered as my parents. I now work as a receptionist in a hotel down here. Stephanie read my words and smiled back at me.

I gestured to her a cup of coffee so we left the park and headed for a nearby café. As we sat down and I ordered coffee thoughts raced around in my head as to where I go from here. I knew that Stephanie wasn't my responsibility and it's not as if she was a child, but somehow I felt that I couldn't walk away from her now, it would be unkind, after all it was me who had decided to make contact in the first place. I wasn't one to do things by halves.

We spent about an hour in the coffee shop, passing info' between us and in that time we had begun to feel comfortable with each other. I had some shopping to do so I arranged to meet her in the park the next day. When I got home I telephoned my mother and told her all about Stephanie. The phone went quiet for a few minutes, and when my mother started talking again she told me about my birth mother. This had never been kept a secret from me so I wasn't sure where it was leading. She went on to say that before I was born my birth mother had given birth to a girl who had been born deaf. The baby had been adopted before I was born and was very settled in her new home. As we both had different fathers and the child was settled it was thought best to leave things as they were, so we were never introduced to one another or any information divulged. This news really shocked me, now it was my turn to be silent. When I managed to collect my thoughts again I heard myself saying, 'Are you telling me that Stephanie could be my half-sister?'

'Well it's possible,' she replied. 'I think you need to investigate more if you can.'

Thinking about it Stephanie did have the same colour eyes as I did, and the same shape face, but all this was a bit too much to take in. I had to get my head around it and anyway Mum might be wrong.

'Why didn't you tell me years ago Mum that I had a half-sister somewhere?' I asked her.

'We were going to but somehow we never got around to it, maybe we were acting selfishly I don't know, we love you very much and I suppose that we didn't want any intervention into our family,' was Mum's reply.

I couldn't sleep much at all that night, I didn't know what to do, all I knew was I had to get it sorted and as soon as I could.

The next morning Stephanie was there in the park waiting for me. I had already prepared what I was going to ask her and had it written down. She read the paper full of questions about where up north she was born and if she knew her mother's name. She wrote back that her mother's name was Janet Sinclair; this was also my birth mother's name. I turned to her and gave her a big hug, we had found each other, we were indeed half-sisters. From that moment on I knew that we could sort things out together, maybe Stephanie could teach me sign language. This was such a coincidence for both of us, a week ago neither of us knew that the other existed. We had so much to talk about but one thing I knew was that now we had found each other, we would never part again.

MONEY FOR MICHAEL
Joyce Walker

Henry hated Fridays. It wasn't because of the heavy traffic he had to negotiate on the way to the office, though that added to his irritation. It was because he knew when he arrived there and sat down at his desk the envelope marked, private and confidential, would be sitting there on top of his other mail, neatly placed under a paperweight by his secretary, Mr H Paton written across it in handwriting that managed to be almost illegible while not being untidy and a painful reminder of the poor father he was to his son.

That day was no exception. He picked up the letter and stared at it long and hard. Should he open it now? No, work must come first. He put it aside and turned to his business mail, though his mind was still with Michael and he was only half concentrating on the job in hand.

When had things really gone wrong between them? Was it when he divorced Ellen, or had it happened much later? It wasn't as if he neglected the boy. They'd spent weekends together regularly for many years and he'd always had the best that Henry's money could buy. As Managing Director of a large company, that meant he could afford to give him the best of everything.

Not that Michael ever appreciated it. Every toy he'd been bought was either discarded unused, or broken within days of receipt, a fact that irked Henry and started the bickering that had grown much worse during Michael's adolescence.

It was the car that caused the current crisis, an eighteenth birthday present, new and very expensive.

'Look Mike,' he'd said as he handed over the keys, 'try to take care of it.'

'I will Dad,' he replied.

Four days later the car was a write-off and his son lay in hospital, injured and lucky to be alive.

He stopped reading his mail and looked about him. It was here, in the office that the storm had eventually broken. Michael had been waiting for him when he returned from lunch, just out of hospital and still pale from the trauma he'd been through.

'And what have you got to say for yourself?' Henry asked, caustically.

The youth shrugged his shoulders. 'What am I supposed to say?'

'You could apologise for being your usual wasteful self and not looking after things as usual.'

'Money,' he replied, 'that's all you ever think about. You don't give a damn that I could have killed myself. Not once since the crash have you bothered to ask me how I'm feeling. Well I'm sick of it. You can take your money and your expensive gifts and shove 'em. Oh, and don't trouble yourself about the cost of the car. You'll get every penny back, even if I have to work day and night for the next twenty years.'

The words hurt more than any slap. Had the expensive presents been a substitute for parental love? If so, they were never intended to be.

For the next two years since the quarrel, every Friday, without fail, that white envelope arrived. Inside, a cheque and a brief statement of what had been paid to date and what Michael felt he still owed.

'Ah well,' Henry sighed, 'time to get it over with.'

The cheque was larger than usual and the letter longer.

Dear Dad,

Please find enclosed a cheque for £500, in final settlement of what is owed for the car. I now owe you nothing at all, except that without your genes I wouldn't have been conceived.

On Wednesday night, I fly out to the States, I don't know how long I'll be gone. I may stay out there for good. I'm telling you this because, despite our differences, blood is still thicker than water and you're still my father.

Your son,
Michael.

Henry stared at the letter for some time. Was the boy trying to offer the proverbial olive branch, or was he just saying goodbye? There was only one way to find out, he picked up the receiver on the phone and punched in a number.

'Ellen, I need to talk to Michael, do you know where he is?'

Three phone calls later he finally tracked him down and asked him out to dinner. The reply was a polite, no.

'It's not that I don't want to, it's just that I have things to do . . . no, don't come and see me off, it'll be bad enough having Mum cry all over me, I'll write when I get settled.'

So that was it, his son was going to the other side of the world and didn't want to see him before he went. Surely, there was something he could still do to show he cared.

He did it in the only way he knew how, by reaching for his cheque book.

With the farewells over, Michael settled down in the departure lounge to await his flight. The letter he'd been handed by his mother intrigued him. Should he open it now, or wait till he'd boarded the plane?

Curiosity finally won out and he tore open the envelope.

The cheque was made out for the exact amount he'd paid Henry over the last two years and the note with it, read simply, bon voyage.

Slipping the cheque into his wallet, he smiled, took his mobile out of his jacket pocket and dialled through to Henry's office so he could leave a message on his voice mail.

'Dad, it's me, just calling to thank you for the gift. Nice to know you have feelings after all, even though you do still only have one way of showing them.'

BRENDA
Mary Long

Brenda was my second cousin, her mother was Gran's half-sister, and she died while having a fit in September of 1941 and she was eleven years old. I have struggled to read what I had written then, as I was only five years old, so part is written by memory alone, but that day I was to look upon Brenda for the last time, has remained in my mind's eye over all the decades that have passed, so I write that day through the eyes of a five-year-old child, and the horror of shadows that crawled all over me.

The sorrow at Gran's was total, the passing of Brenda had cast a shroud of silence save for the sobbing in Gran's living room, the ladies sat making Brenda's shroud because that is what the ladies did, they made shrouds out of flour bags and shrouded the dead. Brenda's bonnet was already made, and lay on the tissue paper on the table, the crystal beads shone all colours in the late September sun, and I heard the leaves gently tap at the window as they fell from the big oak tree. The penny box had been taken out of Gran's Gladstone bag and lay beside Brenda's bonnet, in the penny box were the coins that were placed upon the eyes of the dear souls that 'had gone to meet their maker', tiny silver three penny pieces for babies, farthings for small children, half pennies for bigger children and pennies for grown-ups. I stood looking at Brenda's bonnet and wondered why I would have to look upon Brenda for the last time? I wondered what it all meant; I had never seen the ladies so upset before, and Gran had said that 'I was a big girl now,' and she would take me to see Brenda in her beautiful shroud, and I didn't really want to go, but I wouldn't dare say so as Gran was always right.

I walked to the sitting room and looked through the window, the leaves were falling slowly to the ground, and I thought that when I saw the autumn leaves fall, I would always remember Brenda.

The ladies (Mrs Big Will and Gran) had gone to shroud Brenda, and I went to sit on the bench under the crab apple tree. I knew I would soon be going to look upon Brenda for the last time, Bopa (aunt in Welsh) Tydfil was already dressed in her mourning garments, and all she needed to do was put on her hat. The leaves were falling about me when Bopa Tydfil sat beside me, 'Come little love it is time to go, we will both look upon Brenda for the last time, come now and put on your coat, it is a sad path that we are about to take.' And Bopa Tydfil caught hold of my hand and we went back into Gran's living room, I put on my coat and picked up my gas mask, and walked hand in hand with Bopa Tydfil down Forest Road, the leaves falling about us as we walked.

We walked up the steps to where Brenda had lived, the door was opened and we stepped inside to the sound of wailing. The house was dark as all the blackouts were drawn closed, and by the light of the candle we were shown up the stairs, and the shadows were everywhere, fear welled up inside me and I held Bopa Tydfil's hand so tightly that my fingers hurt. We entered the bedroom and there stood a huge candle in a huge brass candlestick, I almost fainted with fear as all the shadows crawled around the walls, and over the bed that Brenda lay upon. The bed was so high that I had to stand on the footstool, and there laid Brenda, Gran removed the half pennies from her eyes and Brenda looked so beautiful, the crystals on her bonnet and shroud sent beautiful colours around the walls, and I was no longer afraid of the shadows. Brenda's dark hair fell about her shoulders, and there was a smile upon her lovely face, and around her hands Gran had placed Brenda's gold cross and chain. I was lifted from the footstool and Bopa Tydfil and I walked from the bedroom into the candlelight, the shadows followed us down the stairs and to the front door, and then we were out into the evening sunshine.

We walked as the leaves danced at our feet, and I was glad that I had looked upon Brenda for the last time. We walked through the park and it was so peaceful, we sat on a bench and Bopa Tydfil said, 'Well little love, you have seen the beauty of dear Brenda, you have seen the beauty of colours about her person, and one day dear love, you will write of what you have seen this day, you will write of how in the dark days of war, we gave the dead the dignity and beauty to walk through Heaven's gate to meet our Lord, and now sweet love let us walk home.'

And yes the ladies did, and with passion, believe the dead had to have dignity in death.

THE EASTER CANDLE
(For Denis Doyle and family)
Gerard Allardyce

They were so proud and pleased for him. 'They' were his parents and fellow students, the last of his friends at the London School of Economics. He had obtained a qualification in social administration and what in those days was a CQSW, Certificate of Qualifications in Social Work. He had proved to be adept at driving and passed his driving test first time, 'some old Colonel type' of test instructor. It was just another success for the young twenty-one-year-old in our story by the name of Geoffrey Armstrong.

Geoffrey moved onto a housing estate within reaching distance of the Romney Marsh Hospital, a National Trust hospital that was third at the top of the Times newspapers league of hospitals. His posting was in the psychiatric department of the community. The Psychiatric Department was well equipped, and there were two hostels designed for people with mental problems. These ranged from manic depression to Bipolar Affective Disorder. The suite for Electroplexy was particularly well designed and that ward design found itself in an award for the unit from the Prince of Wales Trust. From September to March he worked exceptionally hard and well involving himself with the Consultant Psychiatrist's team of psychologists and nurses both registered mental nurses and community psychiatric nurses. On the strength of a little part time job as a chef at McDonald's on a Saturday evening for six hours Geoffrey had bought a little red Mini Cooper. He was quite the man about town.

The Head of the Department of Psychiatry in Romney Marsh Hospital was Consultant Psychiatrist Tom Hetherington and one day in early April he called in his principal social worker.

'Do sit down Geoffrey.'

The consulting room was spacious and the two men faced each other across the table.

'I am delighted to have you on my team in the department Geoffrey. You came here with excellent qualifications from what I consider the best college in the country and really you have fitted in so well. Two things, I was wondering if you were burning the candle at both ends with the work you do chefing at McDonald's. I personally would like you to end that employment leaving you with your duties here. It served its purpose and you were able to buy the Mini Cooper.'

'Of course you are right Doctor, I'll see to that with a phone call this afternoon.'

'Good chap, splendid and there is a little bit of good news for you. From today I want you to take a fortnight's holiday. Your money will as usual be put in the bank plus your holiday pay. I think you can do with a holiday even if you just do nothing but watch a bit of telly at home.'

'Is that all Doctor?'

'Yes it is Geoffrey and thank you for all the work you have put in to your work these last six months. Happy Easter Geoffrey.'

'Thank you Doctor.'

With that Geoffrey left the consulting room. He picked up a holdall in his office and left the department and hospital in his Mini Cooper. So what now?

Geoffrey decided he would go into the centre of Romney town to see if there were holidays to destinations in the sun like Benidorm, Alicante, Grand Canary, Lanzarote. The list was endless and varied with all places in the Mediterranean enumerated, but he was fed up with the same places. He saw a holiday to Mombassa, hotel, dinner, bed and breakfast for ten days and a safari, price extra and perhaps it was for this reason he decided against the African project.

'Can you help me?'

A lovely girl with a bronze tan called Geoffrey as he looked in the travel agents window. He observed how she had the most lovely blue eyes and dark hair.

'How can I be of assistance?'

'I have come here to Romney to deliver the Easter Candle. It's other name is the paschal candle, I need to deliver this candle to St Anthony's Catholic church in Romney. The person I need is Father Charles, the Parish Priest. By the way my name is Nicole.'

'It's great to meet you Nicole, my name is Geoffrey.'

They shook hands as innocents do when they meet each other for the first time.

'Romney is quite a large town and the Catholic church you are looking for is two and a half miles from here.'

'Do you have a car Geoffrey? It would seem a long walk otherwise.'

It was raining.

'My car is parked just down the road about a hundred yards.'

'That's great Geoffrey, come and shelter under my umbrella.'

'Thank you Nicole. I'll carry the candle if it is too heavy.'

'Will you?' She brightened up and then looked at his pale and drawn face as they walked along the street to the car, Geoffrey having taken the candle from Nicole.

At last they reached the car and Geoffrey placed the candle in the back seat.

They were soon in a twenty mile zone limit when Nicole started to talk seriously.

'Is there a congregational chapel here in Romney, Geoffrey?'

'Yes as a matter of fact there is and I am a member Nicole. The Pastor is very thorough. He has been preaching on St Paul's letter to the Ephesians Verses 1 to 12 for the last four weeks. He will be examining other aspects of the Bible next week after saying he really could have spent six months on the letter to the Ephesians.'

'I am so pleased that we belong to the same chapel Geoffrey. It seems silly delivering this Easter candle. It would seem no shame if it were dumped.'

'Nicole I am disappointed in you. What you have said breaks your trust with the factory you work for making candles in Romney. Our faith does not come into it, we are not firing the first shots in an updated thirty years war. Do you know what the symbols Alpha and Omega mean?'

'Yes Geoffrey, Alpha means beginning and Omega end?'

'That's better. Will you do something for me when we meet the priest in his presbytery and hand over the candle for next Saturday's midnight mass ... be kind and un-provocative.'

'Well Nicole I thought you were kind to the priest and handled the meeting properly.'

'Thank you Geoffrey. The priest was very happy to receive the Easter Candle.'

They were in a coffee bar drinking a Cappuccino each and eating a doughnut a piece ...

'I am a physiotherapist in the local hospital here Geoffrey and I trained in a hospital in Strobolos in Nicosia in Cyprus.'

'That's very interesting Nicole. I am a psychiatric social worker in the hospital,' and then, 'don't you think Pastor Gordon follows very much in the footsteps of John Wesley.'

'And why not and perhaps Geoffrey the Alpha will mark our long trek together in the sharing of our lives until the end, Omega, when we die.'

BLEEDER'S END
T G Bloodworth

Bleeder's End is not so much a village or even a hamlet. It's true, there are few houses amid wooded farmland, but mainly, it's a not so well known beauty spot in the Stroud Valley, about six miles from the town from which the valley takes its name.

It's somewhat off the beaten track and is occasionally stumbled on by summer picnic parties, which with hindsight, would probably have been better for them had they stuck to the better known sights, such as Haresfield or Painswick. I personally have spent many happy hours at Bleeder's End. The pool is clear and almost drinkable. Strangely though there are no fish or wildfowl, and the birds seem awfully quiet, if indeed there are any at all.

It was one glorious summer's day as I recall this strange encounter. I had taken my usual stroll, and to relax had returned to the pool. Dozing quietly in the summer sunshine, I became aware of another presence nearby. Opening one eye, I observed a gentleman on the far bank, eating and drinking from packages he had removed from a briefcase.

He appeared to be a travelling salesman, taking advantage of the weather and his surroundings. On completing his meal, he folded his coat, pillow like, placing it on his briefcase as a headrest. Stretched out in the sun he seemed to be strangely at peace like myself. Such company I enjoyed and decided to make myself known to him. Suddenly at his side, I whispered, not wishing to startle him, I spoke again, louder this time as he seemed not to hear me. His eyes opened slowly at first, then wide and startled. I introduced myself, but he seemed not to hear me and made no effort to reciprocate. All the time his eyes were full of fear which slowly turned to terror as I spoke. I apologised if I had frightened him into waking, but explained my simple wish for companionship.

I suggested he should come home with me and meet my friends, perhaps he would feel better. For some reason this seemed to pacify him, though I sensed he was still uneasy as if he were having a nightmare. I beckoned him to follow, and as I entered the pool he seemed to hesitate. I reassured him there was nothing to fear and that no one was going to hurt him. As he followed me, his head beneath the water, he made that strange choking noise with which I was by now so familiar.

He never spoke again, as his face took on a bloated look. *Just like the rest,* I thought, *now they will come and take him away.* Over the years as I have grown lonely and longed for company in these idyllic surroundings, I've struck up several acquaintances. Strangely though they've never seemed happy when they've accompanied me, and all have declined to make any conversation.

I'm not sure that I'll bother much more, it's the same old story every time. The peace and solitude of Bleeder's End is completely shattered. The pool disrupted and people tramping all over the place. They never seem to notice me during these proceedings and I have long since ceased trying to converse with individuals when there is a crowd.

I heard a man in blue describing Bleeder's End as a place with suicidal tendencies, whatever that means.

But for now I must remain alone, though in summer I find it quite bearable. If you are lonely and like peaceful surroundings, come and look me up in Bleeder's End.

DOUBLE-CROSSED
Cliff Elliott

'Jill?'

'Mmmmm?' Daydreaming, watching the chaffinches on the bird table outside.

'Jill, this is important.'

'Yes?'

'Can you keep a secret?'

Jill swivelled round to face his sister. 'Oh come on! Can I keep a secret? Bloody well no, Louise! You know what I'm like!'

'But could you keep a real secret? Something very important.'

'Really, really important? No way! But tell me, go on.'

Louise turned and faced her sister squarely. 'If this secret was a matter of life and death for your sister - and that's me, remember - would that make any difference?'

'Louise, what are you saying? What is it? What's wrong?'

'What I'm saying, Jill, is that I need to confide in someone. I need to unburden myself to someone whom I can trust absolutely completely to keep it all totally confidential, and who better than my sister?'

'Louise, I'm getting worried. What is it? You can tell me, you know that.'

'Jill, I've done something pretty awful. Something that would get me into terrible, terrible trouble if it ever came out, so it mustn't. It can't. It's not nice, I'm afraid.'

'Then tell me, for God's sake! Tell me! I know I'm a gossip, but I do know how to shut up if it's really important. Go on then. What's it all about?'

Louise turned and sat down at the kitchen table, motioning her sister to sit opposite her. 'You know Sheldon and I haven't been getting on, don't you? Well, of course you do! He's been absolute hell to live with over the past eighteen months or so. You wouldn't be surprised if I told you I couldn't stand it any longer, would you?'

A smile formed on Jill's face. 'What, you're going to leave him? Best way, I'd say. Sheldon's a rotten bastard. Your secret is absolutely safe with me, Jill - I understand completely and I won't breathe a word to anyone!'

'Jill, that's not the half of it! Jill, I've - well …'

'Lou, what is it?' Jill became frantic. 'What have you *done*? What is it?'

'I've murdered him.'

'*What*?'

'No, really. I have.'

'I can't believe that! Come on, please talk sense!'

'I've murdered Sheldon - today, this afternoon. You remember that little phial of Aztec poison that Dad brought from Mexico?'

'Yes ... oh no!'

'And he told us it was completely untraceable. Even with a post mortem, death would look like a simple heart attack.'

'I remember he kept it at the back of his bureau, because he said that very, very tiny amounts were good for arthritis. But I didn't know it was still there. I thought it had been slung out when Dad died.'

'Well, it isn't there any more. I put all of it in Sheldon's flask of tea this morning - before he left in his red Merc' for his business meeting in Hull. He'll probably be dead by now, collapsed over the wheel.'

Jill buried her head in her hands. 'My god, Louise, I just don't know what to say. I can't believe this is happening - I've got to think. Louise! You're a ... a ... murderer! And now - I'm an accomplice! Aren't I? My god! No wonder you couldn't keep this to yourself, Lou - it's so big you just had to share it!'

'There are *three* people in the secret now, Jill. You've seen Angelo, my wonderful new boyfriend. He's on his way over to come and live with me. He's driving over from Pontefract now, in his old grey Morris Minor. There's more to a man than just his car, you know!'

'You don't hang about, do you? But don't you think it will look a bit strange if you take in a new boyfriend on the very day your husband dies of a heart attack?'

'Yes - I can imagine I'll be the police's number one suspect, but don't you see the amazing brilliance of that? It will be so obvious that I will be the prime suspect that they'll reason that if I had really killed Sheldon I wouldn't be silly enough to start to live with Angelo on the same day. Double bluff, don't you see?'

'You are so confident! But the police will surely take you in for some pretty tough questioning. Could you stand up to that?'

'If there's no evidence of any crime, they can't touch me, can they? It's a heart attack - and I've destroyed all traces of the phial the poison was in by burning it and I even buried the tiny amount of ash in a wood a few miles away. I bet even *I* couldn't find it! Just a mo - there, the half-past news on the TV - turn it up!'

'... long delays to traffic on the M62 in both directions this afternoon, due to a serious accident near Brighouse in Yorkshire. Viewers are warned that they may be distressed by the pictures which follow. A car, whose driver is thought to have become incapacitated due to a heart attack, crashed at high speed through the central barrier and collided head on with a vehicle travelling in the opposite direction. Police say the first car, a red Mercedes, the remains of which are seen here, tore out a seventy foot section of the crash barrier. The other car, unrecognisable in this picture, was completely destroyed, but police say it was probably a Morris Minor. Neither driver stood any chance of survival.'

'The Prime Minister completed his cabinet reshuffle today, the third this year. Of the ministers leaving . . . '

A click as Louise reached out shakily with the remote and switched off the set. Silence for a moment, then Louise breathed, 'Angelo's car! That's Angelo's grey Morris! Oh Angelo, Angelo ...'

Jill put her arm round her sister to try and comfort her. She could hardly believe the coincidence that the hated Sheldon, as he had died at the wheel, had taken away her Louise's new love before it had even started. Such poetic justice. She couldn't find words to say to Louise and for a few moments they both sat there together in stunned silence, staring at the blank TV.

They were startled by the sound of the front door being opened by a key and gasped as Sheldon strode into the room, tossing his car keys carelessly on the table.

'Hi, girls. What a day! Dropped my thermos this morning and smashed it so I had to call in at a motorway cafe. Just as well as it turned out - the M62 is all jammed up - big accident it said on Radio 2 - so I just gave up and turned back.' He paused, looked hard at them both in turn. 'Everything OK with you two? You look a bit strange - I'll put the kettle on!'

The sound of a kettle being filled, cups taken out of a cupboard and tapping onto a work top. A fridge door opening. Then -

'Car stopping outside, you two! Hey, it's an old Morris Minor - I haven't seen one of those for a bit! It looks as though it's been looked after ... man's getting out, and it looks as though he's coming here. Shall I let him in, girls?'

WHERE THERE'S A WILL
David Moss

'I still don't see how I can help you.'

The air was filled with the smell of freshly brewed coffee from the machines hissing like steam trains behind the counter.

'Look Mr Cutler.'

'Call me Steve please.'

'Okay Steve, I'm sure something suspicious has gone on. I want you to find out; what and how.' Anna Burns was twenty something, with blonde hair and bright blue eyes, which Steve found very attractive.

Steve said, 'You've already contested the will, the judgement went against you. The change in the will was found to be perfectly legal; dated, signed and witnessed by a solicitor. I'm a journalist, not a private detective. Even if I were I think you're on to a lost cause. I'm sorry.'

Anna's eyes looked tearful, she began to fumble in her handbag, she pulled out a hanky. 'It has been a long standing agreement that after Uncle John died my brother Marcus and I would inherit the manor. We plan to turn it into a hotel. Me managing the catering and accommodation side, Marcus would do the finance and development side.'

Steve put down his coffee cup. 'You have inherited the manor and the grounds.'

Anna interrupted him. 'That's the point; most of the grounds, but we didn't inherit the whole grounds.' She dabbed the corners of her eyes with a hanky. Steve wasn't sure if it was for his benefit. She continued, 'My distant cousin Susan inherited the most important seven acres; with planning permission. We were going to use the money from the sale of the land to finance Woodvale Manor into an hotel. Now I will have to sell my chain of coffee shops. I don't want to have to do that; that's why we're in here. I want you to see what I would lose.'

Steve leant back on his chair. 'What would Marcus have to lose?'

'He wouldn't be able to give up his job at the advertising agency. Without selling that land the whole project may not happen. You will help won't you Steve? You come highly recommended by Vicky; she said you have a nose for investigating things.'

Steve gave a wry smile. 'Including that I found out she was two timing me.'

'She's my friend and she still thinks a lot of you,' Anna said.

'Maybe, but I'm not going out with her anymore.'

Anna slid her hand across the small table towards his. She leaned towards Steve. 'No you're not are you. You will help me, won't you?'

Steve didn't say anything. Anna's hands squeezed tighter as she said, 'I want to find out what that sly bitch and her good for nothing husband are up to.'

Marcus Burns' office at the advertising agency was just how Steve imagined it would be; a modern design with a vivid green carpet which extended all the way into the office. Marcus was standing by an expensive looking coffee machine from which came the same lovely aroma that took Steve back to his meeting with Anna Burns the week before.

'It's the same blend that Anna uses.' Marcus handed Steve a cup of coffee. He wasn't like his sister at all; he was taller with dark hair and designer glasses. Steve had been there for about half an hour, so far he really only backed up what Anna had said.

Marcus walked over to his desk. 'I've already done a lot of work on how we'd market the place.'

Steve looked at the drawings. They were good, they made him feel that he would like to stop there. He looked up from the plans. 'Can I ask you a personal question about all this?'

'Ask away. I've nothing to hide.'

'I get the feeling you couldn't wait for Uncle John to pop his clogs.'

Marcus laughed. 'No it's not like that at all. Uncle John was in on the hotel plans from the beginning. You see he didn't want Woodvale Manor to end up as a dilapidated ruin. It's been in the family for a very long time. But times change, Uncle knew it's going to be increasingly difficult to carry on without doing something drastic. He decided to apply for planning permission on some of the manor's land, so it could be sold in order to finance the hotel. But suddenly he changed his will without telling Anna and I. We didn't find out that Susan will inherit the land with planning permission until after he died.'

'That's why you contested the will?' Steve said.

'Yes, we've no idea why he appeared to change his mind. As far as we know Susan and her husband Tony only began to see Uncle John six months before he died, before that there was no sight or sound from them.'

There was a moment's silence while they drank their coffee. Steve said, 'What was the cause of death?'

Marcus smiled and shook his head. 'I wondered that myself, but it was through long standing illness. Uncle John regularly went to the doctors. He managed to give up smoking cigars, which surprised me. His determination not to give up booze killed him in the end. Maybe they put pure alcohol into his drink!'

Steve smiled. 'Even if they did, it doesn't explain why he changed his will.'

Marcus looked out of the window. 'Actually Susan and Tony only visited him about three or four times before he died.'

'I think we can rule out murder. This leaves us with a bit of a dead end. No pun intended,' Steve said.

'Would it help if you saw the house? Anna and I are going up there this weekend.'

'It might do,' Steve replied.

Steve found Woodvale Manor off a quiet country lane surrounded by trees. As his car approached he could see it was a brick built pile with a mixture of mullion and larger windows. This was because the house had largely burned down during the nineteenth century, Marcus had explained to him in a potted history of the place.

Inside Anna was packing away photographs into a large cardboard box. 'Hello Steve.' Anna straightened up, her hair was tied back but a stray lock fell across her face. She pushed it back with her hand. 'Uncle John was very keen on photography or I should say being photographed. There are loads of these things in every room.' She handed Steve an arm full of photograph frames.

Steve looked at each one. Uncle John had been every inch the portly tweed suited country squire. In two of the photos he was even wearing a deerstalker and toting a shotgun. Steve noticed in every photo he was smoking a large cigar.

'Put them into that box would you?' Anna pointed to a box on the floor. As Steve put the photographs in, he saw one was a picture of Uncle John, Anna and Marcus standing at the front of the manor. Steve grinned and showed it to Anna. 'Oh yes, I remember that day. It was taken quite recently.'

Steve looked at the photo for a long time. There was something about it that he couldn't put his finger on. 'Can I keep this?' He showed it to Anna. She stopped and gave Steve a long look, the corners of her mouth turned slightly upward. Steve felt she'd misunderstood his meaning. 'It's for the investigation.'

Anna kept her look. 'Of course.'

Marcus came into the room. 'Do you want to see the building land?' Steve nodded. 'We can take my car.'

Marcus directed Steve along the lane surrounding the estate. Anna who was in the back seat giving an additional running commentary suddenly shouted loudly, 'Bloody hell. That was Susan and Tony in that car.'

'What! Are you sure?' Marcus said.

'Yeah certain. What the hell do they want?'

'I think that's your answer.' Marcus pointed towards a large white sign sticking up out of the hedgerow. It read, *exclusive housing development with telephone number.*

Steve rang the number and made an appointment to see Susan and Tony Angel. He found out they were property developers. True to form according to Anna they were maximising profit by using cheap labour and doing most of the work themselves. Their office was a small shop off the main street in the nearby town.

Steve was now sitting in the reception with Susan who appeared to be doing all the filing and phone answering. Susan was younger and prettier than Steve expected she would be.

'Would you like a cup of tea Mr Cutler?'

'Yes, thank you that would be nice.' Steve watched as Susan disappeared into another room. On the table in front of him were some guides to buying property in Spain. Susan reappeared and put the cup onto the table.

'I don't know if you like sugar so I put two sachets on the saucer. Tony is on the phone, but he won't be long now.'

A few minutes later the door opened and Tony greeted him. 'Sorry to keep you waiting Mr Cutler. Take a seat, we may as well get down to business. What kind of property are you looking for?'

'Something in Ibiza, but not in the main resorts.'

'Okay. How much do you want to spend?'

'Oh sorry, yeah about ninety thousand pounds maximum.'

Tony's eyes followed Steve's to a framed poster on the wall. 'Tony Angelino. That's you isn't it?' Everything came together in a flash in Steve's mind. 'You're a hypnotist!'

Tony was smiling. 'That's right Mr Cutler. Let's drop the pretence shall we. I saw you in the car with Marcus and Anna.'

'You hypnotised Uncle John to give up his cigars. That's why he wasn't smoking in the photo I showed Anna. While he was under your influence you suggested he should change his will in Susan's favour.'

'I don't know what you mean about the photo, but yes you're right. I am Tony Angelino. I had a very successful career, until things started to go downhill in Britain for hypnotists. So I moved abroad to Spain mainly, there I met Susan. She became my wife and manager. Then one day we met someone who was kind enough to leave me something in his will in spite of his family's objections. It's all he ever wanted to do. I hope I'm not boring you Mr Cutler, but your eyelids are drooping. You're feeling drowsy, that will be the sedative Susan put into your tea. You see I just want you to listen to the sound of my voice . . .'

THE UNSUNG HERO
D F O'Doherty

I often take short breaks in Scotland. The grandeur of the Highlands and the crisp mountain air provide a welcome respite from the frenzied activity of a bustling city. I also like meeting people, especially those characters with an exciting and colourful background.

I remember well my recent break in the Highlands. The hotel looked out onto a narrow sea loch, its shimmering waters reflecting the towering mountain on its southern boundary.

That first evening, I struck up a conversation with a white-haired, elderly man who was greeted as 'Duncan' by the hotel staff and some of the guests.

'You seem to be very popular and well known,' I remarked.

'Aye! You could say that,' he replied, 'before my son filled the post, I was the hotel manager here. Since I retired, I can't seem to keep away from the place,' he grinned.

'Perhaps you're not impressed with modern day management,' I smiled.

'In my day,' Duncan continued, 'one got by with good organisation and common sense. Now, one is expected to hold a university degree in hotel management, business studies and computer technology.'

A few minutes later, Duncan excused himself and left to attend a granddaughter's birthday celebration. It was then I noticed a little balding man, probably in his eighties, dressed in tunic and kilt, a pair of buckled patent leather shoes and a row of service medals emblazoned across his chest.

As an ex-serviceman myself, I identified the Military Medal, the Africa Star and Clasp, the Italy Medal and the usual World War Two medals. The little man was talking animatedly to a group of people seated across the room. I wondered why and in what circumstances he was awarded the Military Medal.

The following evening, my luck was in. The little man carried over his drink from the bar and sat down at my table.

'On holiday?' he queried.

'Just a short break.' I replied. 'The traditional tunic and kilt always catches the eye. I see you are wearing the Military Medal.'

He looked around the room and leaned forward. 'It happened in Italy during the Second World War,' he said, lowering his voice, 'would you like to hear about it?'

'Of course,' I smiled. I bought him a beer and settled back to listen to his story.

'During the Italian campaign,' he began, 'my battalion held a position at Venafro near the lower slopes of Monte Cassino. I was part of a seven man patrol sent out on a reconnaissance towards the German lines.' He paused and looked at me closely to see if I was listening. 'OK?' he queried.

'Yes!' I answered. 'Please go on.'

Again he looked around, rather furtively I thought, then continued his story. 'Lieutenant Baird was the patrol leader and I, a sergeant was his second in command . . .' he sipped his beer appreciably and continued, 'it was dark when we started out along a narrow track. You could hardly see your hand in front of your face. A few bushes gave some cover to begin with and then we crawled forward on our bellies in strict silence. I wasn't too happy about the lieutenant; a young whippersnapper straight from officer training school. You know, the *gung-ho* type who would cheerfully lead you to your death.'

'Yeah! I know the type. We've all met them,' I muttered.

'We got so near the German positions we could even hear them talking. The lieutenant made a rough survey of the enemy forward positions and then we headed back down the hill. Half-way back all hell broke loose. Mortar bombs exploded all around and the track was swept with rifle and machine gun fire. Two of our young soldiers were killed instantly. We dived off the track and tried to take cover as best we could.'

'My God!' I breathed, 'they must have monitored your movements and set up the ambush knowing you had to return down the same track.'

'That's right,' the little man agreed, 'the lieutenant was wounded in the neck and shoulder but despite this, managed to crawl slowly down the slope. At last - it seemed like an eternity, we came in sight of our forward positions.' He paused and slowly sipped his beer before resuming the narrative, 'To reach safety, we had to cross about two hundred yards of open ground. Lieutenant Baird was in a bad way and didn't have the strength to travel any further. I shouted to the lads to make a run for it, then threw Baird over my shoulder and ran across the clearing to safety. How we managed to survive in that hail of bullets I'll never know. The other three didn't make it.'

At that moment, Duncan came towards our table carrying a glass of wine.

'Excuse me,' muttered the little man, 'I just remembered an urgent appointment.' He got up from the table, scurried out from the room and disappeared through the main front door.

Duncan sat down in the vacant chair. 'I see you've been talking to wee Willie Brown,' he remarked.

'Wee Willie Brown!' I repeated.

'Aye!' Duncan continued. 'The wee lad with the Military Medal. I'm sure he told you all about his heroic deed at Monte Cassino?'

'Why, yes he did,' I answered, 'he must be the local hero in the village.'

'Hero, my foot,' growled Duncan. 'Willie was never a hero and a poor excuse as a soldier. He was usually in trouble for being insubordinate, getting into fights and going AWOL. He must have spent more time in the *glasshouse* than on military duty.'

I sat there with my mouth open. Did Duncan resent Willie's Military Medal? Yet on the other hand, he could be telling the truth. 'I don't understand,' I stuttered, 'why would he make up such a story?'

'Oh, he didn't make it up entirely,' said Duncan, 'the story of the patrol is true. But there are two major falsehoods. Wee Willie was a lance corporal, not a sergeant and his daring deed saving the life of the lieutenant was also completely false. A young nineteen-year-old soldier carried the patrol leader back to our lines. But, just when they reached safety, a sniper's bullet pierced the lad's helmet. He died instantly.'

'But where was Willie during this time?' I asked.

'Trying to save his own skin.' Duncan growled. 'The lieutenant and Willie were the only survivors.'

'But surely, the patrol leader knew what happened and . . .'

'He did, indeed,' said Duncan, 'but he was unable to tell anyone. He spent three months in a coma in an army base hospital, then two months in a convalescent unit. It was going on six months before he rejoined his unit.

A gullible company major recommended Willie for the Military Medal. Perhaps, he should have delved a little deeper before he made that decision, but then, in the heat of battle such an administrative lapse is understandable.'

'Yes, I agree, especially when the battle lines changed so rapidly,' I said.

'When the patrol leader returned to his battalion,' Duncan continued, 'he tried to put matters right, but failed. The War Office was very sensitive to adverse publicity. The fact that the wrong man was decorated and a young private died an unsung hero would have been meat and drink to the media. No, the true facts were swept under the carpet and Wee Willie could go on bragging about his heroic deed for the rest of his life and do you know, he's told this story so many times that he's actually come to believe it.'

'What I don't understand,' I told Duncan, 'how come you know so much of the details? Did Willie tell you?'

'He didn't have to tell me,' he murmured with a wry smile, 'I was Lieutenant Baird, the platoon leader.'

WHEN ONE DOOR CLOSES
Dorcas Walker

'Here's another one, Betty,' called Sam Growlett as he sat in the open doorway of their stationary caravan. 'Forget about the telly and come and have a look. It must be at least four berth and have an end bathroom. I told you this was one of the better parks, didn't I? Even if it is a bit pricier than some we've been at, you must admit, you do get a better class of people. Just look at the brand-new four-by-four, must have cost a bob or two, that one.'

Heaving herself reluctantly from her comfy chair, Betty waddled over to the door and peered out, screwing her face up against the still bright sun of the early evening. 'Can't I get any peace?' she grumbled. 'You always want me to look at something just when I've settled down to watch Corrie - and for heaven's sake, will you stop yer staring. Anyone would think you'd never seen a decent van in your life before. It's always the same wherever we go. One of these days . . .'

'Just weighing up the neighbours, love. No harm in that now, is there?' Sam leaned back against the door frame and drew a last pull from his cigarette stub before grinding it into the grass under his heel.

'But do you have to make it so obvious?' Betty complained. 'You're about as discreet as a vicar in a brothel.'

Sam shrugged his fleshy shoulders and carried on with his covert observations. 'It's a good thing we got here when we did, old girl. There's hardly a vacant pitch left. Still we've been at this game long enough to know what bank holidays are like. You have to be quick off the mark if you want something decent.'

'You're not wrong there Sam.' Betty nodded her agreement. 'You know, I think this caravanning lark is the best idea you ever came up with. It's been grand just moving around from place to place these last few months.'

'So you don't miss the old homestead then?' he asked.

'Miss a poky little two up and two down in a grubby run-down terrace? You must be joking! Besides all this fresh air is doing my chest the world of good. Rest and relaxation - seems just the thing to me - not to mention all the nice people we get to meet.'

'That reminds me, got talking to him next door.' Sam leaned his chin on his palm and looked pensive.

'Oh yeah - and I suppose by now you know his whole history and even his shoe size.'

'Don't be daft. I don't ask personal questions.' Sam protested. 'Anyway they're called Bill and Jenny. He's a taxi driver and she's a nurse. They've not been married long and they've a couple of teenage girls from previous marriages - bet they're a handful.'

'I suppose so, but like I said, it's none of our business so I'm going back to my old telly - I've got to catch up on Eastenders before we take a walk down the club tonight, that's if you still want to go.'

'Course I do - wouldn't miss it for the world. Talking about telly, luv - see that blue van at the end of the row ...' he gestured with a sideways nod of his bald head, 'they've got one of them fancy flat screen kind - no thicker than a deck of cards, it is!'

'Speaking of decks and you're not with a full one at that, when are you going to sort out that cruise I've always wanted?'

'Soon, luv, soon. I'm working on it,' Sam promised, grinning all over his round, sun-reddened face.

Later, as they sat near the exit of the smoke-filled clubroom, Sam kept on with his running commentary about their fellow caravanners. 'Packed in like sardines tonight, luv,' he said, 'and just look at 'im over there flashing his cash like he was Rockefeller.' Sam nudged Betty in the ribs and received a less than loving look for his trouble.

Turning her head to glance in the direction he indicated, she nodded in agreement. 'Looks like he intends to enjoy his holiday. That roll of notes would choke a horse, some people have all the luck, don't they?'

'He's from that van in the top corner - you know the one with the twin axle and the new-looking awning.'

'Trust you to know all the details,' Betty laughed as she took another swig from her near empty glass, 'get me another vodka, luv, and don't drown it with tonic this time. That last one was like gnats you-know-what. If I can't get a bit tipsy when I'm on holiday ...' she called after his retreating figure, 'then when can I?'

Next morning Betty groaned as bright sunshine found its way between the curtains and pierced her red-rimmed eyes.

'Oh God, I feel awful,' she moaned and turned over to face the wall.

'Well you can't say I didn't warn you.' Sam's lack of sympathy was evident. 'But you'll feel better after a cup of tea and a bit of breakfast, sure as eggs is eggs - and while you're sorting yourself out, I'll take a walk down the shop for the paper. Maybe have a bit of a stroll while I'm at it. It'll help clear my head - I downed a few pints meself last night so you're not the only one who's suffering.'

Sam sauntered down the rows of caravans, waving cheerfully to families setting off in their cars for the nearby beaches and beauty spots, he paused to exchange pleasantries with the taxi driver from the next van. 'No, we'll just have a quiet day and stop here,' he told him, 'poor old Bet's got a king-size hangover after last night. I've left her sleeping it off. Anyway you get away and enjoy yourselves. Have a nice day,' he called after them, 'and don't do anything I wouldn't do,' he grinned.

Late that afternoon, Sam was roused from his usual nap by the sound of angry voices outside.

'Two hundred bloody quid gone - just like that!' he heard one man say.

'Where did you leave it?' asked another, as Sam raised himself from his chair and hurried to the open door. Outside stood a tight group of people, among them his neighbour, Bill the taxi driver and the fellow they'd seen flashing his money about in the club the previous night.

'Left it in t' caravan as I always do,' the man was saying, utter dejection on his face and slumped shoulders, while behind him a scrawny little woman, whom Sam took to be the man's wife, stood wiping her tearful eyes on the sleeve of her bright red track suit. 'Me whole holiday money gone,' she wailed, 'and it was hid under the mattress an' all.'

Sam had heard enough. He stepped outside quickly and hurried over. 'Been some trouble, lads?' he asked, concern clearly evident on his face.

'Two hundred quid nicked from his van.' The taxi driver gestured towards the victim.

'Was it a break-in?' Sam queried and received withering looks from the assembled group.

'Van wasn't locked' said the taxi driver. 'You can't have been at this game long or you'd know there's an unspoken rule with caravanners about not locking doors. Might have to change now but it's a throwback to times when people trusted one another. You looked out for one another and never did the dirty on your own.'

'Probably not a caravanner that's done it then,' Sam said shortly. 'Probably some kids - though I did see a couple of dodgy looking characters hanging around,' he added, 'they had a tent over there on the camping field yesterday. Most likely be them, I'd say.'

'Right lads, let's go and have a look at those guys,' said Bill and several of the men growled in approval.

'Oh they're long gone.' Sam shook his head in regret. 'I saw them pack up and leave a couple of hours ago. If only I'd known what they were up to.'

A wail of anguish from behind him halted Sam in mid flow and he turned to see Betty's white face, her hands clasped to her open mouth in horror. 'Sam, Sam,' she stuttered, 'my gold watch - I left it on the side table last night and my mother's rings - they've gone!'

'Oh Betty love. Looks like there's been a couple of low lives on the rob. Must have had your rings away when we went up the pub at lunchtime. Nicked this guy's cash an' all, they did.' Sam's face was bright red with anger and indignation.

'Mind your blood pressure, old lad,' said Bill, 'don't want to give yourself a heart attack. What's done's done. I reckon all we can do now is call in the coppers.'

'And what's the flaming point of that?' Sam said. 'Those scumbags'll be miles away by now and the cops wouldn't even know which way to go after them.' Sam shook his head in despair and patted Betty's quivering shoulder. 'Come on, old girl. Let's get you back to the van. A drop of brandy's what's called for, but I'll tell you one thing …' he tossed the words back to the assembled company, 'you won't catch me stopping here one more night and that's a fact.'

Later that day, as they drove into a caravan site a few miles further up the coast, Sam and Betty were unusually quiet, each thinking their own private thoughts.

'Do you think we'll ever go back there, Bet?' asked Sam eventually. 'I mean after all that happened, would it be wise?'

'Oh I don't think so, Sam, though it was nice of the park manager to apologise the way he did when it wasn't really his fault. What did he say - nearly a thousand pounds in cash and the jewellery? Not a bad day's work for somebody, eh?'

'Yeah, a cool thousand, old girl. A thousand nearer to that luxury cruise you've been harping on about.'

'Stash it in the usual place, did you?'

Sam nodded in satisfaction. 'A cool thousand - not to mention a nice new telly - no thicker than a deck of cards!

'Right!' he added as he drew to a halt at his allotted pitch, 'let's get settled in and then we'll see what the neighbours are like …'

No Comment
Jan Whitfield

Every time there was a jewel robbery in the city the old bill called on me, inviting my *help with their enquiries* - a nice little phrase they use when they're pretty sure you've done the deed, but haven't got enough evidence to pin it on you. They have to satisfy the Director of Public Prosecutions they've got a good case, you see, or it's all thrown out of the window. So I made sure they never had anything they could use against me. I was too clever for them. I always had a cast-iron alibi - and a smart lawyer.

The interview room at central nick was no different from all the others I'd been in - a table, four uncomfortable chairs, a tape recorder and a stony-faced uniform standing to attention by the door.

Me and my brief, Alfred Hooke, sat on one side of the table and a couple of so-called detectives on the other. You know the scenario. The old nice cop - nasty cop routine. Nasty shouts and screams at you, then Mr Nice gets you a cup of tea and a fag, thinking that'll soften you up.

'You've got your alibi for last night?' Hooke had queried before we went in and I nodded a reassurance. 'Right,' he said, 'if they question you about anything else it's *no comment.* Remember that and you can't go wrong.' He spoke in a whisper, even though we were alone and I could see the pound signs glittering in his eyes behind thick pebble glasses.

He knew I was guilty of course, but as long as he got his percentage of the proceeds, he didn't give a damn. Hooke was as bent as a paper clip. I knew plenty of decent blokes banged up inside for a lot less villainy than Hooke had committed over the years.

'All right. I know the drill well enough by now,' I protested, 'it's not as if it's the first time, is it?'

Although they pulled me in from time to time and had their suspicions all right, I don't think the cops could really come to terms with the idea of a mere slip of a girl, as Inspector Fraser called me, being the best in the business when it came to breaking and entering. It's the old chauvinist thing. But I didn't get the nickname Katie the Cat for nothing, did I?

'This job has your hallmark all over it, Adams.' Fraser (he's the nasty one) was saying through gritted teeth. 'I know it was you, so why don't you just admit it and we can all get some sleep.'

'Not me Mr Fraser,' I protested, assuming a wide-eyed innocence, 'I told you, I was with my latest fella last night. We had a meal at Luigi's. You know, that new Italian place in the precinct. Do you like Italian food, Inspector? They do a lovely fettucine bolognese and . . .'

'Never mind that,' Fraser scowled, 'what about after, where were you after Luigi's?'

'Went straight back to his place. Must have been just after eleven. I swear it on my mother's grave.'

'Oh yeah? So what's this boyfriend's name and where does he live?' Fraser glowered. 'Let's see what he has to say.'

Jack Masters would swear the Pope was Moslem if he'd thought there was a bob or two in it for himself! You know the type, dark and good-looking in a shifty sort of way with monkey's eyes, sly and sliding in a lean face. If ever there was a money-grabbing shark it was Jack-the-Lad and what he earned he kept, his wallet stuffed with notes.

'You shouldn't carry that much cash around,' I warned him when he'd flashed a wad of twenties at Luigi's last night, 'it's not safe.'

But would he listen? Jack didn't trust banks. 'Too easily robbed by folk like me,' he laughed. He wasn't really my type but for an alibi he was totally dependable - as long as the money was right.

Of course, it had to look real. I made sure I was seen with him a couple of times a week over the last month, establishing a routine, letting folks get used to seeing us together. We went to Luigi's last night, just as I'd told Fraser, then took a cab back to Jack's flat. He picked an argument with the driver over the price to make sure he'd remember us and then deliberately kicked up just enough racket to disturb old Ma Henshaw next door, before I slipped out the back way. So, knowing my alibi was as safe as houses, I rhymed off his name and address with complete confidence and sat back.

'My client has answered your questions, Inspector and accounted for her whereabouts. I take it she is now free to leave,' Hooke smirked.

Fraser stared at him with undisguised loathing. 'Not until I've checked out this so-called alibi,' said Fraser firmly, 'I may wish to question her further. Just wait here.'

Hooke's soft, manicured fingers beat an impatient tattoo on the table as we waited.

'Cut that out!' I growled. 'You're making me nervous.'

'Don't worry. You're fireproof. Just stick to your story for last night and no comment for anything else. OK?'

It was a good hour before Fraser looked in again. I'd expected him to look a bit put out when my story checked out but instead he was surprisingly cheerful. 'So you stayed all night with Jack, Kate? You didn't slip out at all - say around midnight?'

Around midnight I was climbing through a skylight window in another part of the city, but I had the perfect alibi didn't I? Bought and paid for. I didn't fancy Fraser calling me by my Christian name though. There's something not quite right when the police suddenly turn matey.

I glanced across at Hooke, who gave me an almost imperceptible nod. 'No way,' I insisted, 'I never left his side until eight o'clock this morning.' I leaned back on the chair and treated Fraser to a smug grin, but surprisingly he only grinned back at me.

'And you're willing to sign a statement to that effect?' he said.

I nodded.

'Right then, I'll just go and get it typed up.'

I turned to Hooke as the door closed behind the inspector. 'Fraser seems very pleased with himself. I don't like it.'

'I've told you. Don't worry.' Hooke sounded cheerful enough but nothing could dispel my odd feeling of uneasiness and I was relieved to see Fraser back with the statement in his hand. One quick scrawl of a pen and I'd be out of this dump. You wouldn't see me for dust, I decided and I'd be keeping a low profile for the next few weeks.

Fraser laid the typewritten sheet in front of me. 'Before you sign this Kate, are you still standing by the fact you spent the night with Masters? That you were with him between, say, midnight and two am?'

'Absolutely positive.' Alarm bells were going off in my head, but there was no way Jack would grass me up, not with the kind of money I was paying him. I hesitated briefly, then signed my name with a flourish.

Inspector Fraser folded the statement almost lovingly and nodded in satisfaction.

'So you won't be surprised to know that Jack was found this morning with a six inch knife in his chest. Time of death estimated round one am.' Fraser cleared his throat noisily. 'Katherine Mary Adams - you are charged with the murder of John Philip Masters. You do not have to say anything but it may harm your defence if you do not mention, when questioned . . .'

The familiar words of the caution hit me like a series of hammer blows and I felt the colour drain from my face. I half rose from my chair, then slumped back. 'No comment,' I croaked.

MANDA BEACH
E Harris

The fair-haired youth walked past the Australian War Memorial and turned the corner.

Twenty-four hours later, when his distraught parents had searched for him unsuccessfully, they decided to call the police. They in turn found no trace of him, it did not take them long to make a thorough search of Canberra.

The two little girls ran gleefully into the water then splashed around swimming. The Dumont sisters were nearly the same age, one was ten and the other was eight, they had dark, curly hair and a cheerful manner. They were both wearing a blue and white striped swimming costume and looked like twins. After a while they came out of the water and lay down on their towels in the dunes.

The fair-haired youth walked further along the beach. Sweat was pouring down from his brow into his eyes. He wiped it away with the back of his hand and blood mingled with the sweat.

The man driving the old utility truck with the blue cattle dog in the back braked and stared after the lanky blond youth, who kept walking along the side of the dirt road in the bush. He was walking at a normal pace and the back of his white shirt looked clean enough so the driver shook his head as he thought he must have imagined the blood stains all over the front of the boy's shirt. So the driver went on towards the beach.

He released the dog who made a bee-line for the dunes. The man had just taken his fishing tackle out of the back of the truck and laid it on the ground when he heard his dog howling pitifully. He rushed towards where the howling was coming from and found the bodies of two young girls who had been slain. He fainted.

Constable Collins looked up as a middle-aged man stumbled towards the counter, followed by a blue cattle dog.

The murder hunt was launched immediately. There was a great flurry of reporters, the description of the blond youth was published in all the newspapers. There were special editions devoted to the 'Manda Beach Murders', the horrified public were moved with sympathy for the grief-stricken family. Their emotions reached a peak when the headline, 'Arrest imminent' appeared.

Sergeant Tom Hailey opened the front door, he walked wearily into the kitchen and sat down heavily at the table. His wife Jean said nothing, she deftly made a pot of tea. He remained silent as she poured him a cup. She waited quietly, looking at his greying crew cut and tired, unshaven face.

After a while he murmured, 'What's the bloody use . . .'

Still she said nothing. When he had left the house at the crack of dawn that morning he was brimming over with excitement and pride: with his pals he was going to arrest the Manda Beach murderer.

At last Tom said to her, 'We got the little bastard. Jim started bashing him up but we pulled him off. Not that we didn't feel the same ourselves. Over the car radio they told us not to go back to the station because of all the reporters. Bill answered and said that he didn't see why the reporters shouldn't see that we'd done a good job. After all, the whole country was waiting for this arrest. The captain yelled back at him to shut up and stay put until the ambulance arrived. An ambulance? We hadn't asked for an ambulance. When it got there the captain rushed over to us with two fellows in white outfits. They extricated the little bastard carefully from our vehicle as though he was made of porcelain. They strapped him down ever so gently in the ambulance and gave him a shot of something in the arm to put him to sleep.

I stayed in the back of the ambulance with him and one of the male nurses. The captain rode in the front with the other one, the rest of the boys followed us. We stopped at a place that looked like a private hospital. They carried him inside on a stretcher, we were told to wait outside.

After a few minutes, a limousine pulled up in front of the porch. Four blokes got out, real smart suits, big smiles. They followed the captain and us into a sitting room. The captain told us everything would be fine, we were just going to be placed under oath to say nothing to anyone about the arrest. The smart suits helped the captain tell us that it was 'A matter of national security.'

The marine stepped neatly aside as the First Secretary knocked on the door and entered the luxurious office. 'Your excellency, the police have found your son.'

The American ambassador stood up and pressed his hands down on the desk. 'Where is he?'

'He's in Sydney, Sir.'

The night had been long. The First Secretary continued reading the document out aloud.

'... the solemn undertaking that my son will be committed for life to an institution for the insane in the United States of America ...'

They had spent hours discussing this agreement with the Australian representatives. The American ambassador nodded wearily and leant forward to sign the document that had been placed on the desk before him.

The next day the American ambassador left Australia discreetly. He was replaced by another one.

The young, blond man stood at the top of a cliff overlooking a beach in California. He watched some children playing on the water's edge. Then he started picking his way down the cliff path to the beach. Nobody saw the knife in his hand: except for the three children, the beach was deserted.

THE CRIME
Shirley McIntyre

It wasn't long before the orderly came with Geoff's twice-daily drugs. There had been a couple of periods during his time 'inside' when he decided that the medication was not necessary. He had pretended to swallow the tablets while the orderly was still in his room, but what happened afterwards was so terrible he accepted that the drugs were for life, like his prison sentence, he no longer resented the small yellow capsules, in fact they had become like a reliable friend, a crutch.

He let his mind wander as the effects washed over him. They did a good job calming him but they often caused hallucinations too. His lids felt leaden so he gave in. As he closed his eyes he saw a vision, could that be Angela? No surely not, it looked very like her but she was absolutely stark naked. Sure enough there she was playing the guitar and singing John Lennon's 'Lucy in the Sky with Diamonds', it would not normally be her way but there was no denying it, he'd recognise her anywhere with or without clothes. Energised into action, Geoff was soon up there with her. They were singing a duet and somehow resembled Sonny and Cher but without a stitch of clothing on! Then half-way through 'I got you Babe', they were transported away to a beach, their nakedness magically covered, Angela's with fur and Geoff's with feathers. Arm in arm they got into a pea-green boat and as they sailed into the sunset with the sound of the song 'The Owl and the Pussycat' ringing in their ears, Geoff thought he had never known such absolute contentment. He was finally happy and free with his beloved Angela. At that moment it really did not matter a jot that he was transformed into an owl and she into a cat, all he wanted was to stay like this for eternity - content, soporific, carefree.

Without warning, his euphoria burst like a balloon as a huge wave engulfed the boat and they were swept away gasping and spluttering on the undulating waves, the salt water stinging their eyes and nostrils; but quickly he remembered, it was going to be OK after all, now that he was an owl he could fly away from this danger, not only that, he could become Angela's hero. Revitalised by this thought he flapped his soggy wings frantically, grabbed hold of Angela by the neck and, although she was by now miaowing very loudly indeed, he clenched her in his talons and flew away.

All too soon the delusion faded and when Geoff opened his eyes, unhappiness overwhelmed him as he absorbed the familiar surroundings, the bed, chair, scruffy little rug and of course his beloved radio. It was always like this, hallucinations so vivid he could not help but believe they were true and the knowledge that it was all just a dream could either bring gut-wrenching disappointment like today, or relief if it had been a very bad trip.

Even the night brought no peace as he was constantly plagued by dreams. If they were bad it was wonderful to wake up and look forward to the heavy cloak of depression lifting, all the same, more often than not he found the humdrum routine of his days disturbed by certain objects, words and thoughts that suddenly ricocheted him back to his muddled dream world. He had to shake his head violently to distinguish fantasy from reality. There was one memorable occasion when he truly expected the small, shag-pile rug at the side of his bed to continue to quote the poetry that had so disturbed his sleep during the previous night! He even remembered the rug's sickening words:

Been down here so long I'm an expert on crime
With you lovely lot, all doing your time
I've heard it all, the boozing, the crack
Causing violence and murder, and stabs in the back
And there you were smeared head to foot
With flesh and blood and brain and gut
Bumping your bird off is common enough
But chopping her up, well now that's nasty stuff
We know what it's like when you lose your cool
When loose tarty slags make you look like a fool
But there you were smeared from head to foot
With flesh and blood and brain and gut
So OK you killed her and that I'll excuse
Finding her like that'd make me blow a fuse
But to spend those long hours just chop, chop, chopping
Is beyond me mate and for that you want topping
And there you were from head to foot
With flesh and blood and brain and gut
What would have happened if the cops hadn't come
Would you just simply have legged it and run?

> Why not use your head before making that mess
> Got rid of the proof and made the pigs guess
> *But there you were smeared head to foot*
> *With flesh and blood and brain and gut*

Geoff shuddered; all too often his sleeping hours were punctuated like this, forcing him to relive his grisly crime in a variety of ways. He often awoke to feel the smooth wood from the axe causing his palms to sweat and the metallic stench of blood in his nostrils making him retch.

He thought he had always loved Angela. From that first moment of their meeting in the library at York University in 1969, he desperately hoped that she would be the solution to his anger problems. Certainly he fancied her, God who wouldn't with those voluptuous curves and fiery red hair, it soon became obvious that she felt the same and they immediately hit it off. Her vivacity and good humour struck a chord from a happier past and she seemed to be just what he needed so, despite his occasional black moods, they got on so well they were soon inseparable.

Angela was aware of Geoff's bad temper, as she had witnessed it on several occasions with their fellow students. He was very intolerant of noise and chaos so he found the untidy, boisterous house he shared with four other students quite unbearable at times. This was one of the reasons Angela agreed to share a bedsit with him for their final year. Although he had never lost his temper with her, she did tire of his dark moods and silences and he convinced her that this would all change if only they could move in together.

They deliberately found a bedsit away from student land and for a while this seemed to work. The other residents in the three storey Victorian house kept themselves to themselves and Geoff felt happy for the first time since he was a child. He only wanted Angela and he quickly let it be known that they were happy just as a couple - refusing invitations to parties and nights out, they stayed in every evening watching TV or making love. Occasionally at weekends they might go to the cinema or for a drink but always on their own.

Eventually this insular lifestyle began to pall for Angela so she started making arrangements to go out with old friends, but she never enjoyed it, she kept thinking of Geoff's stony face as she left him in their dingy little room. She knew only too well how a couple of hours out with friends could bring on a week's sulking from Geoff, so in the end she decided it was not worth it. Angela was still so bored though; after all she was only 22. She wracked her brains for a way to release her pent-up emotions.

Even as a child, Angela had aspired to become a writer so, with Geoff's encouragement, she managed to pick up an Imperial typewriter from a second hand-shop for ten shillings. Geoff would go along with anything that would keep Angela away from other people. Now she spent her spare time rattling away on it in the corner of their one room. All too soon Geoff began to feel left out.

That's all she ever does, he thought, *she never has time for me now and the noise of that bloody typewriter is enough to drive anyone mad.*

It was true Angela had become completely absorbed in her novel; she was a romantic girl and saw herself as the heroine of her story. She tried to include Geoff in her writing by asking him to proof read her work but he only managed a few pages before Angela became incensed by his smirks and wisecrack remarks. They started to row more and more and on many occasions Angela tried to finish the relationship but it was no good, Geoff cried and begged, vowing he could not live without her, he pleaded with her to stay, threatening suicide if she left. Angela could see his jealousy and melancholy were getting worse week by week so she dare not risk leaving him in case he did try to kill himself, but she was getting desperate, he had even managed to put a stop to her writing. She had come home from a lecture one lunchtime to find her beloved typewriter gone and she was categorically told she could not get another, explaining that the noise from its clattering keys hitting the roller made him feel ill.

A few weeks later Geoff announced that he was going to visit his parents the following weekend and Angela welcomed this respite from his constant attentions and questions, which were becoming more and more accusatory as time went on. His latest gripe was that she was seeing another man and it did not matter how much she reminded him that they spent all their spare time together, he would not leave it alone and had taken to going through her pockets and handbag whenever he got the chance. The anger and jealousy were getting to such a pitch he had to find out the truth before he went crazy. He told Angela he would be catching the 5pm Sunday evening train back from his parents' but he actually intended to return on the Saturday instead. She had no reason to suspect there would be any change in his travel arrangements as he had always been a stickler for routine and punctuality, in fact this was another of his traits that had intensified over the past weeks, he was constantly checking his watch and was obsessed with keeping their days to a rigid timetable. She had even noticed a barely discernible tic under his left eye when they did not quite sit down for dinner at precisely 7 o'clock each evening.

As Angela waved goodbye from the window that Friday afternoon she felt herself relax for the first time in months.

Now it was Saturday night and he was back. He tiptoed up the stairs and gently turned the handle of the door to their room and there before his very eyes was Angela in bed with another bloke. Although he had expected it, he felt completely stunned by the sight of them together naked. His head was spinning, he thought he would be sick and time seemed to stand still. He wondered if he might have actually passed out because when he looked at the bed again there was only Angela, nobody else. He looked frantically round the room but there was definitely no sign of anyone else there. It was too late, the voices had started and above her ear-piercing, hysterical screams, he heard them chanting, *kill her, kill her, go on do it now, kill her, kill her, go on do it now.* He had no choice, he was compelled to put his hands around her throat and squeeze very tightly indeed.

BLOOD WILL HAVE BLOOD
Tony Macmillan

The head fell and landed on the floor. Although Guy moved his foot smartly he could not prevent a red stain marking his shoe.

Putting down his paint pot and brush, he picked up the wandering head. Carefully he cleaned off the smudge of paint on his shoe and looked with strong dislike at the face. The unwinking eye of the puppet stared back at him. Guy did not like this one.

He was a clever artist and the faces of his puppets all had a strong personality, but recently even the good characters were beginning to take on a somewhat villainous look. He could not think why. They seemed different from his normal puppets. Had he perhaps given their creation less thought and care since Tracy came into his life? Or did he paint badly on nights when she was not with him, like tonight?

The finished models hung on a rack that stood in the corner of his bedsit, between the foot of his bed and the cracked window. Not much light reached there and, whenever he turned to look at them, the impression was of evil. It made him uneasy.

His Punch looked particularly raffish, with more than a hint of the Hunchback of Notre Dame. Snow White dangled there with a look of decayed innocence. She seemed to be constantly turning her head as if someone was touching her from behind. Next to her Dopey still wore his vacant smile, but his hands were always out of sight. There was in their faces more than he recalled having painted, especially as they were not meant to terrify. The rack in the corner was close to the window, but surely the draught could not account for the perpetual slight movement?

Now, as he looked at them, he wondered if the evil he saw was in their faces, or in his hands. Was he the one who put his own dark side into them? His thoughts depressed him and he decided to paint no more tonight.

He put the lids back on the paint tins and cleaned his brushes. Going across to the bed he picked up his coat, put it on and straightened the pillow. As he did so he visualised himself thrashing about on the bed. The ridiculous thought made a shiver run up his spine. He carefully did not look behind him to the shadowy corner.

As he went out, slamming the door behind him, he could tell that the resultant breeze caused the hanging figures to shift and rustle. He heard what sounded like a whisper and he paused outside the door, but decided against going back in.

As he went downstairs there was no noise from any of the other rooms. The whole house seemed dead and only he was alive. Outside the moon shone doubtfully on the damp street and the fitful wind wrinkled the puddles. He hunched his shoulders against the drizzle and walked to the corner.

Undecided he looked both ways. The only welcoming light he could see came from the windows of his local, so he crossed the road and hurried towards the warmth. Suddenly he needed company.

But the bar was as quiet as the street outside. The few customers gazed at their drinks with a heavy dislike.

He turned with his drink and saw Brian in the far corner waving at him. He never realised that Brian came here or he would never have dared bring Tracy. He stood for a moment, unsure whether he really wanted to talk to her husband or not. The sight of Brian awakened feelings of guilt that he would have preferred to ignore. Tracy's thighs were a haven of forgetfulness.

Reluctantly he walked across and saw to his horror that Brian was crying.

'What's the matter?'

'It's Tracy.'

Guy went cold and he sat down heavily.

'How do you mean?'

'It's my puppets.'

Brian, like Guy, made puppets and gave professional shows. His puppets were enormous, life-sized, filled with sawdust and incredibly heavy. He had enlisted Guy's help for one of his shows and they had both finished the evening in a state of sweaty exhaustion. The puppeteers lugged the gigantic figures into position with all their strength and, at the same time, spoke the lines.

Most of Brian's shows seemed to include battles, and the puppets were armed with wicked looking weapons, which they used to hack and stab at each other with furious abandon. All the time the manipulators were declaiming ferocious blank verse from some long forgotten age.

The children who watched his shows ignored the verse with its mighty sentiments and glorious chivalry, but cheered themselves hoarse when the battles started. As it was difficult to tell which side was which, they cheered each clash with marvellous impartiality, while their accompanying adults winced.

Guy avoided the possibly dangerous subject of Tracy.

'What's the matter with the puppets?'

Brian took a grubby handkerchief out of his pocket and wiped his eyes.

'I told you Tracy couldn't stand my puppets, didn't I?'

'I don't think so. No, I don't think you did.'

'She called them monsters. Why couldn't I build small ones like you do? I didn't know she'd even seen yours. Well that's what she says.'

Guy spilt a little of his drink.

'What do you mean? What's the matter with her?'

'Nothing. She's all right. Well, she was when I saw her last.'

'Has she gone then?' Guy did not know whether to be glad or sorry. If she had left Brian, there was always the chance she might finish up with Guy.

Brian took a deep breath and gazed blearily round the bar. Guy thought he looked very drunk.

'I think she hated me too.'

'I didn't know that.' Guy was embarrassed. He always felt that to be told someone's confidences somehow put you in their debt.

Brian got wearily to his feet and made his way across to the bar. He came back slowly with more drinks. He slumped down in his seat again and Guy waited, knowing there was more to come. When it did, it was with a rush.

'I should have known I suppose. Over the years she got worse and worse. She never let up. Mind you, she never complained at the extra money I brought home. It was just the time I spent with them. Making them and rehearsing. She said I thought more of them than I did of her. And she may well have been right.'

Guy nodded. 'It does take up a lot of time.'

Brian sat for a while staring at his drink. His fingers drummed restlessly on the table. Then he looked up at Guy again. For a moment Guy wondered if he suspected where Tracy had been spending her evenings.

'I used to spend more and more of my time with them. She was out anyway. I don't know where.'

Guy moved uneasily but Brian didn't seem to notice.

'I began to tell them my troubles. They couldn't answer but I was sure they sympathised with me. They seemed to nod at me.'

Guy thought of his own puppets shifting and whispering back in his dim room.

'Tonight it was.'

Guy jumped. 'What was?'

'Last week I'd just finished making a new model. It was one of the best I'd ever made. Blackbeard. A marvellous villain. Very lifelike. Huge creature with a great bristling beard and a gigantic sabre. It almost made me shiver to look at it. Then tonight I came home from and it had happened.'

Guy waited, but Brian seemed to have gone into a trance.

'What had happened?'

'She'd gone you see. Well, I thought she had. There wasn't any supper anyway. So I went out to my workroom. There wasn't anything else to do and when I got there she'd destroyed them all. Every last one of them. It must have taken her the whole day. There was stuffing and cloth everywhere. The mess was awful. There wasn't a complete one left. I couldn't even find any bits of Blackbeard anywhere. He had completely vanished. And he was my best. All gone. And Tracy too.'

Guy wondered which he was mourning the most, his puppets or his wife.

'I know how you must feel.'

'Do you? Do you?'

Brian's eyes filled with tears again. Guy's depression was curiously lifted by finding someone in a worse state than him, so he started to try and cheer Brian up.

This effort consisted in them getting progressively more drunk as the evening wore on. Brian drank with a quiet desperation and Guy kept up with him, partly friendship and partly guilt. Although he did wonder where Tracy had gone.

By the time they were out in the street after the pub closed, they were reduced to holding one another up. The rain was still coming down steadily, driven by a strong wind and the clouds were scudding across the face of the moon. Brian pushed Guy away.

'I can manage. On my own.'

'Are you sure?'

Guy let go of him and he staggered a little before he started down the street. He took only a couple of steps before he stopped and leaned against the wall. Guy moved to help him, but was stopped by Brian's imperious gesture.

'They were nearly human you know. I loved those puppets. All of them.' His voice grew louder and he again raised one hand. 'I would have died for them. And they would have done the same for me.'

He pushed himself away from the wall and went along the street at a shambling run. Guy watched him go and saw him turn the corner in safety. Then he could no longer hear Brian's footsteps and he was alone.

He thought of his puppets rustling and jogging on their rack and he did not want to go home, but there was nowhere else to go. Reluctantly he crossed the road.

As he climbed the stairs he became aware of a jumbled noise. He could not make out where it was coming from, but when he reached the landing he knew it was from behind his door.

The whispering and the rustling were worse than usual. He was tempted to run downstairs and out into the night, but his feet would not turn. He had to go in. Guy opened the door and the noise welled out at him. Quickly he turned on the light.

His puppets seemed to be moving more wildly than ever and for one terrifying moment he thought they were alive. He stood not daring to move. They bobbed towards him and retreated. Several of them were on the floor. Snow White was on the bed and Dopey lay on top of her. Her smile was wider than usual.

Then he saw the window was wide open and the night air was whipping the curtains in frenzied writhings.

He felt the sweat on his forehead and smiled in relief. Forcing himself across the room he picked up one of the prone puppets.

'Idiot. I am an idiot.'

He put out his hand to pick up another and then stepped back in sheer horror. Lying slumped on the floor was Tracy with a wide gash at her throat and blood all over her face.

As he stood, unable to move, the body rolled to one side and the head, detached, rolled wetly towards him. He looked down to see a red stain on his shoe.

There was a sudden noise from the window. As he turned he saw a huge figure with a bristling black beard standing there. He could see the flash of a long sabre as the figure began to move towards him.

Behind him, on the bed, he was aware, briefly, of Snow White laughing out loud.

FROM WAKING
Mark Thirlwell

Footsteps, Doppler past my door. Cellarage thoughts two steps at a time rise and enter. Yesterdays scurry along the skirting and nest in the pool of yellow day. Something within me senses this movement, this part of me, this familiar squirming of consciousness, and through closed lids I see them. Crawling over, around and under each other they appear to be one moving mass, one form, one animal. Some, far from their beestings, continue to grow. Others, parts of the whole, the whole that was becoming who I was, stare at me with black, scabrous eyes. They want to be fed, suckled, their grey-pink scratching limbs reach out for me, their dumb mouths squeal a silence that pierces and fishhooks the paper-thin skin of my little death.

A too loud television, in its insistence, bleeds through the bricks, mortar, plaster and paint and drips its colours into my head. It mixes with my waking thoughts and splices an unnatural and freakish edit. Senses kick, stir, I fight it wanting the dark, the sleep. The mass wants me, it moves closer on me, I can feel its weight behind me, beside me, beneath me and around me. The sun grips the house in its day and stretches its beams, twists and creaks its fabric ad imitating, my yellowing bone ivory house, its frames and panes strain and are thrown open to the noise on which they hunger.

I lie unable to move, knowing that the faster I run the fatter and uglier they become. So I lay still, feeling the underbellies of each, velvet their coldness over me, around me, inside me. Each of my vertebrae crack wide, fissures, each bone like the grinding of teeth is shaved closer to each marrow, each marrow is filled with their liquid malignity. In me they feed, turning over, fattening and filling any void in them, with me.

The faintest of breaths, neutral in temperature and indistinct of source, moves the skirt of the curtains. A needle of sunlight injects the room, cells of skin, dust, exoskeletons of creatures long dead, drift in the streamed vein of light. The needle minutes its way to me and with its prick of heat, skewers me filling me with a grain of something, something lost, half-forgotten. Then as usual, in the acid womb of my stomach another one of them begins to grow. Sensing this birth the pink-grey mass surrounding me, becoming me, makes room for another, another one to feed on my senses, the chaos of my waking.

I feel the seed split and grow as I have felt all the others inside me grow. What will this latest of conceptions needs be, what will it crave? Might this one be the last, the one to swallow me whole? I feel it in my veins, the feel of it squeezes the chambers of my heart so it drums to their bat, and my ribcage spreads and calcifies. This crumbling bone cage of me becomes its home and my gaol. It spreads from my stomach up across my chest, like the coldest of syrups swallowed. It rises up, a slow burning, ulcerating vomit enters my gullet expanding it, making me gag. I wretch as they pass my tonsils and enter my mouth, where they deposit their sloughed skins. These bitter, acrid tasting excreta pack and fill my mouth, pushing my lower jaw as far as it can go, bringing water to my eyes as I scream out in my stifled, choking muteness.

Like tics they feed on me, not my blood, but the essence of who I am. Slowly, daily with each dawn they change me, reconstruct my inner selfscape. Through taut half-closed eyelids I can still see the mass, its capillaries grow pinker as they, and it, feed and join, turning me as grey as the dust of the still, greyer quiescent shade.

The stagnant yellow pool of day turns a shade darker and as it does so the mass, the whole, stops its forage of me. I do not see them leave me, just feel their weight lessen, lighten as they scurry again in my periphery, away from me. I cough, splutter and spit out the grey they left me with and swallow lungs full of cool night air. Their voices that had pierced me from my sleep fade, as in the twilight settled grey, under the window sill, I crouch, I curl, my nocturnal self. I sleep, safely quilted until the white of day wakens my senses.

TWO FOR THE PRICE OF ONE
Zoe French

An owl hooted slicing through the black night. The girl walked nervously along the path in the marshes. She knew the way, but it did not stop the terror racing through her. How many people had lost their lives going through here? There were some tall rocks in the middle that you had to go around. This she was dreading and she was drawing close to them. The rocks stood up tall and sinister, you could hide anything in them, and she had to get around them.

Although she was scared, she couldn't turn around and go back, she had to go on to get to her home. The mists were swirling around her, adding ghostly shadows everywhere. There was a glassy look to the marshes, except where the bubbles sometimes came to the surface and broke with a squelching noise. The girl was now very close to the rocks; there was a sudden noise that had nothing to do with the marshes. The terror which had subsided slightly returned in full force. Who or what was there? It was a scratching noise, like a cat sharpening its claws. She heard the murmur of a voice. Someone was there. Who? Reaching the rocks she went around them carefully, dreading what she might find. She had reached halfway around them when she came upon a strange sight. A young man was there with a huge black panther. The young man had his arms around the panther. The girl stopped, amazed. The young man asked her name.

'Jenny,' the girl replied. 'What's yours?'

'Jack Roberts,' answered the young man, 'and the panther's name is Arthur. He is very friendly and wouldn't hurt a fly. Unless someone should hurt me. I've grown up with him you see.'

'I'm on my way home and have to go through the marshes to get home,' said Jenny.

'Would you like me to walk home with you?' questioned Jack.

'Yes please, if you would not mind too much and it isn't out of your way?'

'Come on, Arthur will look after both of us.'

They had just left the rocks and were walking along the path when a dark shape loomed up out of the marshes blocking their path.

'What on earth is it?' asked Jack.

'I don't know,' whispered back Jenny.

Suddenly the shape took the form of a large man who was now stood in front of them waving what looked like a gun at them.

'Where are you kids going this time of night?' the stranger asked them.

'I don't think that's anything to do with you,' stated Jack and put his hand out to Arthur, but there was nothing there. Arthur had a mind of his own and had already decided to find out what the man was carrying in his hand. No one had seen him move, because the night was so dark and the panther being black, blended in with the shadows. Jack had an idea that Arthur was investigating the situation and so did not call him.

'You two on yer own?' asked the man with the gun.

'Why, what's it got to do with you?' asked Jack.

The man moved closer to them.

'I should stay where you are,' said Jack having spotted Arthur just behind him and slightly to the left. He had seen his yellow eyes shining in the dark.

'An' what would yer do about it on yer own? I've got a gun see and the marshes are famous for covering up dead bodies. Here I have two for the price of one.'

A cry of dismay came from Jenny hearing this, she knew it was true. However were they going to get out of this alive? She couldn't understand why Jack didn't seem so bothered. The man cocked the gun and took aim. The panther had heard enough to tell him Jack was in danger. He sprang at the man's back knocking the gun out of his hand and onto the pathway. The man staggered, then slipped into the marsh headfirst. There was a gurgling sound as the marsh sucked him down. Jack and Jenny were paralysed with fear and intrepidation. What would the police say?

'Don't touch the gun,' said Jack. 'They might recognise him by the fingerprints on it.' Taking a clean handkerchief out of his pocket he picked the gun up by the end of the barrel.

Reaching Jenny's home he dialled for the police. When they arrived there were statements to give and the gun to hand over.

'If it's who I think it is,' said Inspector Kilter, 'it was an escaped convict who has already killed three people. We will know for sure when we take the fingerprints off the gun. You were both very lucky, but for Arthur you would both be now at the bottom of the marshes.'

Arthur hearing his name mentioned lifted his head and put it on the inspector's lap to be rubbed. As it turned out it was the escaped convict. Inspector Kilter told them there had been a good set of his fingerprints on the gun.

Three months later the bells of the church rang out in Jenny's road. Waiting at the end of the aisle was Jack all dressed up in white tie and tails and top hat, waiting for his bride to be to walk up the aisle on her father's arm. The organ filled the church with music of the Wedding March as Jenny glided down the aisle towards him in a beautiful white crinoline dress and a long white veil. The church was packed, they all wanted to see the wedding of two very brave people. Arthur was there of course, sporting a blue satin bow tied around his neck and sitting next to his friend Jack, although now he would have two to look after. The wedding vows were taken and there wasn't a dry eye in the place. Everyone thought what a lovely couple they made as they walked down the aisle as husband and wife with Arthur at their side.

THE FIRST DEFIANCE
Sandra MacLean

The fairground was busy and full of noise from the chattering people. Screams and laughter could be heard from the direction of the various machines. Dreary lights flashed in his eyes from the various stalls that monotonously littered the field. Cheerless music resounded in the desolate corners of his ears. The place smelled of cigarettes, petrol and candyfloss.

A tramp came running up to him and asked him for some change. After searching his pockets to find chewing gum and rolled up tissue paper, he eventually grabbed some tens and threw them in the direction of the tramp. A squeal elicited from the throat of the tramp as he scurried to pick up his prize. Dax shook his head and walked to the nearest stall where a gypsy woman thrust a plastic gun into his face. He assumed it was loaded with plastic pellets she wanted him to shoot at cardboard rabbits marching behind her. Dax reached into his breast pocket and shoved the photograph he produced into the woman's face. The gypsy's face fell as she realised she wasn't going to secure a sale. Nonchalantly she glanced at the picture and shook her head. Dax ground his teeth in irritation and returned the photo to his pocket. He gained a cigarette from his other pocket and lit it with the Zippo lighter Vance had given him a few years back. It still bore the inscription: *To Dax, Five Years, Many More - Vance.*

Breaking from the monotony of the fairground he turned onto the busy road; a Porsche screeched past him followed by a puttering '55 Morris Minor. Its bright headlights shone in his eyes and highlighted the deep circles encased there. A café stood across the road: a bright neon light flashed the words 'T-Time Café'. His tongue suddenly felt very dry and he could almost feel the individual pores of his taste buds sticking to the roof of his mouth. He crossed the road and entered the café.

The air was thick with cigarette smoke; two men and a boy inhabited the place and the men were seated on cheap plastic seats. One sat rather precariously: Dax smelled the alcohol as he passed. The kid stood playing a pinball machine that looked like something from a 70s movie. The kid completely ignored Dax as he passed: he was too engrossed in his game. Dax noticed one of the men was playing with his fingernail, which was half hanging off. He shook his head at the predictability of the café and walked to the counter to order a coffee. After paying, he took his coffee to a plastic table beside the window and sat down with relief when he realised it didn't wobble. He deposited both elbows onto the table, rested his chin on his clenched fists and let his eyes wander outside. Countless people strolled past, eyes as black as dusk. No one seemed to notice the eloquent full moon that floated above them; not one person noticed the strong tree that stood proudly down the street which, from this angle with the moon piercing through it, looked as though it had skeletal fingers reaching for the innocents at the fair. Dax hated society today and wondered why more people didn't look towards nature and notice the beauty surrounding them. The irony of what Dax was thinking did not hit him at first.

He drank his coffee in two swift gulps. It wasn't until he stood to leave and felt the pressure of the gun against his groin that the irony of his thoughts hit him. Dax chuckled to himself as he left the café. The man with the hanging nail looked at Dax, shook his head in disgust and stuffed the nail into his mouth.

Dax re-entered the street and looked at all the bustling people. This is where she had last been sighted.

She was the daughter of his boss. Violet was her name, Violet by nature. Until she'd started college, started wearing white make-up and acting all depressed, listening to sad music and talking of death. Started moaning that her father had treated her badly; that he'd been too possessive of her since her mother had died giving birth to her brother. Both mother and boy had died. Haemorrhage and asphyxia respectively. Dax remembered how his boss had been afterwards. He'd never seen a man in so much pain. The double funeral was lavish and even his enemies had attended out of respect. His boss had never really recovered and Violet became more isolated.

Dax had always liked Violet. In fact, he'd always had a wee 'thing' for her. Not that he'd let his boss know. No one was good enough for his precious Violet; certainly not one of his hench-men and Dax didn't fancy trying out concrete boots. He'd had to sustain his admiration in secret.

Dax had watched her as she played the dutiful daughter and provided polite dinner conversation for her father's business guests. Watched her kiss her father on the cheek as she retreated to her room to play music. He saw her as she stood on her balcony smoking a secret cigarette and then discarding it into the undergrowth as she heard someone enter the room. Her life had seemed restricted and empty, until she started college when she started hanging out with an older man. Dax hadn't liked the look of him and Vance asked him to find out his story. Dax'd tried following the guy but he seemed to live in shadows. Dax could only follow him so far then he'd almost disappear out of sight. Violet wasn't forthcoming with information about him: when questioned by her father she just blushed and looked at the ground. To her father, he was her first known defiance.

Dax'd followed them one night they'd gone out together. They'd gone to some night-club. He'd heard Violet and her father shouting about it the next day. She'd stayed in her room after that, but Dax'd seen her on the balcony and she'd had a black eye. He'd felt angry and guilty that he'd caused her father to hit her, but he had to remember where his ultimate loyalty lay.

Looking back, Dax realised this was what'd sparked everything off. She'd become more withdrawn, then eventually left.

His boss was furious. He didn't like not having her in his control. He vowed to find her, hence Dax being deployed. He'd been looking for two weeks now and his employer was getting agitated. Dax could understand him being annoyed that his daughter had run off, but she was 21 now and entitled to her own life. Dax couldn't quite understand the level of possessiveness. It resembled control of a wife. Strange, towards a daughter.

Dax turned a corner to continue his search. He showed a few more people her picture but no one seemed to recognise her. It was while lighting another cigarette, leaning against an alleyway, that he saw her.

She looked pale and was dressed in black. Her lips bright red and glossy, her hair sheer silk down her back. She was alone. Haunting the streets. She looked round then walked further into the alley, her heels clicking the concrete. Dax ducked into the shadows and followed her. He wanted to see where she was staying and who with. Vance wanted to deal with her himself.

He lost her. Right in front of his eyes, she disappeared. Dax stopped. There was no sound in the alley except for the now distant noise of the fair. Dax inched forward as quietly as he could. There was a doorway ahead, she could've gone in, but Dax hadn't taken his eyes off her. Surely he would've heard a door slam? He moved quickly towards the door and it opened to his touch. It creaked as he pushed it wider and he stepped into the room in front of him.

The door slammed shut behind him. Dax turned to look at it in puzzlement. He hadn't closed it and there'd been no breeze; the door was heavy to push and Dax could see grooves in the dust where it had scraped along the floor. He examined the hinges, which were rusty: there was no way the door could have closed on its own. Dax frowned and looked for a handle. There was none. The door was smooth and melted into the wall. Dax was trapped.

He heard a noise behind him. It sounded like a muffled groan. Dax looked round at the room. It was huge. Dax couldn't understand why he hadn't noticed such a large building before; it looked small from the outside. In the centre of the room was an impressive marble staircase. It was bound by elaborate wooden railings and fanned to both sides near the top. He heard the groan again. It was coming from a door to his left. As he approached the door the groaning intensified accompanied by a shuffling sound. With a slight pause perpetrated only in anticipation of what lay behind the door, Dax reached out for the handle and turned it. Nothing. It was locked.

A crash sounded from behind him. Dax turned around in panic. There was nothing there. The moaning through the door stopped abruptly. There was an arctic silence around him. He rushed to the centre of the room where he found his gun lying at the bottom of the stairs. His hand automatically went to his pocket, which he was surprised to find empty. The gun was bent from its journey down the stairs and bullets were scattered across the floor. Dax was confused as to how his gun had vanished from his pocket and had somehow been thrown down the stairs.

He realised he was no longer alone. There was someone close by panting very heavily, waiting to pounce, waiting for him to turn round so they could make their move. The breathing came faster and sharper: the Devil was waiting to strike.

Dax spun round. There was no one there. He was alone after all. The breathing was his. The loudness of it was his panic. He needed to keep control. He took a deep breath to compose himself and ran up the stairs to confront who had stolen his gun. There was no one there. The stairs were empty. At the divide they gashed left and right, ending in red velvet curtains which when pulled apart revealed two walls: two dead ends. The stairs went nowhere.

Below him he heard a door open.

Each stair creaked as he tentatively moved his way back down. Adrenaline was gathering in his belly and slowly filtering through his veins. He could feel his heart beating faster and he tried to concentrate on breathing slowly to keep himself calm.

The door to his right was open.

He couldn't hear his footsteps as he crossed the floor. Time sped up in sympathy with the rapidity of his beating heart. Before he knew it his hand was on the door. He pushed it and walked inside.

Everything changed. He felt himself being grabbed from behind and then felt the sophoric coldness of polar skin against his neck and icy teeth piercing his throat. They felt like frozen needles. His vision blurred.

He was in a room. Vance stood over him, only younger. He looked down at his hands only they weren't his. He recognised them. They were Violet's; he was looking through her mind; seeing her memories; she was showing him her life, looking for understanding. The vision changed and Vance was carrying her into her bedroom. As Vance laid her on the bed he was dictating that her door was to be kept locked. He said things were going to change. Dax looked down at her hands and saw the bandages on her wrists. His vision blurred with tears.

Alteration. Vance was shouting about a boy. Dax felt the stinging blow to her cheek as Vance struck her, saying he was putting guards on her door. He saw himself from her eyes, from the balcony. He was hiding in the bushes thinking she couldn't see him. He saw himself standing behind Vance, staring at her as Vance told her she wasn't going to her friend's party that night.

He felt her entrapment, unhappiness; felt her pain of always being watched. He could see himself now, through her vampire eyes. His skin drawing paler as his life-blood was drained. He looked pathetic: a vessel of liquid. His vision snapped back into his own eyes and he saw her face through the haze of his approaching unconsciousness. He could hear the dry slowing of his nucleus and felt the lumbering weakness of his body as it slumped towards the floor.

In his last living seconds, Dax reflected on the futility of his life and on the impact of control over innocence. As he heard her strident laughing, he thought of Vance, his boss, her father, and realised he would be her next victim. She was seeking revenge for her pitiful life.

THE END TIME PROPHECIES
Marcus Vorment

Hello, my name is Simon Joyce and I wish to tell you of my very strange and unusual experiences while in a state of trance and psychic meditation.

It all started with just a few books from the library, you know the sort, psychic development, the chakras, etc, etc.

I have always been interested in delving deep into the human psyche, but have not really taken the opportunity until now. I started with twenty minute sessions in meditation. At first there was nothing special in this, but as time went by I began to relax into it more and develop a very real sense of my other being, a new spirituality that was being awakened so to speak.

Meditation gets good when you begin to visualise. Have you ever tried the one where you travel to a castle in a forest to meet your spirit guide? Anyhow, about five weeks into this practice I found that my mind would wander to places that I had indeed not planned on at all. I began to travel into space. This could prove to be quite frightening, as sometimes I seemed to have trouble returning to Earth while in this state. Each time that I meditated I appeared to travel further and further away from the Earth.

I don't know much about astronomy at all, but I started to realise that with each session I was getting closer to the planet Mars. I could see the red planet with two moons, and I could also see its polar ice caps. The visions continued for about two weeks until eventually I was in orbit above the planet at high speed. Once I saw huge dust storms raging across the surface of Mars.

It was at this point that I started to be lowered to the planet's surface. I panicked as I looked back into the night sky for signs of Earth. I found that I could no longer tell which of the heavenly bodies was my home planet. The dust cleared and I saw the southern polar ice cap of Mars with its deep crevices and icy gorges. I landed and stood on the ice sheet as a spirit being, immune from the incredible cold that would have otherwise killed me if I had been there in my earthly body. I walked across the tundra of frozen water, ice and carbon dioxide for what seemed like half an hour, trying to figure out my purpose for being there.

To my shock and astonishment I came across what seemed to be a dilapidated monastery with most of its windows blown out. I was amazed, did NASA know about this?

Ice dust blew across the floor of the building in the gentle breeze. Struggling to see in the dim light I saw some sort of a humanoid form sitting at a desk over by the far window. Life on Mars! I could not believe my eyes! The figure wore a monk's habit and looked very much like the Grim Reaper. I have to say that I did indeed feel quite frightened. I had to approach this most morbid figure. I could not see the face as the hood was almost completely closed up. The figure seemed to be writing something down on scrolls.

It beckoned me over to it without saying a word. I nervously tried to ask it who it was and why it was here and it replied by some form of telepathy. Its reply was, 'I write the prophecies of the end times and the horrors which are to come.'

I said to it, 'But why here? Why on Mars?' To which it offered no response other than to beckon me to observe the writings on the scrolls.

The writing was done with quill and ink and was not written in any language that I had ever seen. I noticed that under the desk were many hundreds of scrolls in boxes, so how many prophecies could there be? Looking back at what this figure was writing, it seemed that I was given the ability to understand the text though the language was unknown to me. I shall tell you what the text said:

2021 AD. England is finished! Hear the words of warning, England is finished! The proud founder of empires is now laid bare as a third world nation. Two out of every five people are either criminals or drug addicts. Three out of every five cannot read and are considered to be completely unemployable. The kingdom has crumpled to dust; anybody that still has the means to leave should leave, and go quickly. Yes I say, flee to other lands while there is still time. Flee to them before England's disease reaches their peoples and they too become proud of possessing vileness of attitude.

O England, O England, why do your people not speak truth from the heart no more? Why does everybody act and mime? All your greatest leaders have abandoned the sinking ship, to live in other lands to escape the corruption and lawlessness that has ravaged your nation. I looked upon the streets of England and saw no coherent person anywhere to be found, instead there were only people senseless through the use of drugs and substances while their children wandered aimlessly searching for better role models and finding none.

I felt myself well up with anguish and spoke to the spectre, 'No, how can this be? You must not allow it! This is my England that you are talking about!'

The spectre just pointed at the scrolls and motioned for me to read on:

2027AD. Mass cannibalism takes place in England. The vile and the ungodly no longer have anyone left to feed and house them; all the administration has left for other lands. The once proud criminals have now begun to feed on each other. These are the same people that shouted with joy when decency fled the land and raised their voices in triumph when the government fell. Now it is they who are in sorrow, they who are in mourning now that there is no longer any state handout, and though they have always avoided work, there is none now they have finally decided that they want to work.

The vile and the ungodly break into government and social security buildings, hoping to find a clerk who can give them money or food. But there is no one to be found, all have fled across the seas to escape from the drug users, work shirkers and criminals.

Suddenly I understand what I was reading. I could see it in my mind's eye; they were the equivalent of the punk rockers and the gangster rappers of our time, baseball caps and bad attitudes and all the rest of the trimmings that go with these sorts of people. Poetic justice would eventually come to knock at their door for all the problems that they had caused others over the last forty years or so. Protected initially by political correctness, now all of their former smirking was laughing back at them. They had mocked and jeered at decency and now decency was jeering back. There will no longer be any people left to mollycoddle them because they have all left England to escape the scumbags.

2035AD. The entire Earth is gripped in total war, extreme Islamic terrorists have access to nuclear weaponry and the whole of the Middle East is under attack by China. The European super army has invaded Britain with permission from the exiled British government and is forcing British drug addicts and dropouts to fight the terrorists on the western Saharan front. The United States of America is all but a ruin now, decaying from within, due to corruption, crime and delinquency.

The European super armies of France and Germany join the fight to aid the Russians against the advancing Saudi army while the South American alliance have joined in the fight on the side of the Middle East. Everywhere there are millions dead.

2039AD. Thousands of the Earth's elite try to leave the Earth to escape from the vile and the ungodly. Their space galleon 'Nebraska Sunrise' explodes in a catastrophic nuclear drive failure, just two hundred miles above the Earth. There are no survivors and thousands of people on Earth die from the resulting radiation.

This indeed looked like very bleak prospects for mankind but the spectre pointed to another scroll, therefore I read on:

2114AD. The last of the human survivors have gathered together one last time after generations of war, disease and famine. Everywhere streams are poisoned; everywhere the water holes produce nothing but death!

The humans are now making their last stand in Africa's Ngorongoro Crater, the very same place where the first humans emerged, huddled together against the ferocious predators on the crater's perimeter. Now here they are again, facing the very same animals with nothing but sticks and stones. But this time it is different, these animals are wraiths, empowered spirit beings of their former extinct selves, they have pursued their quarry mercilessly across the face of the Earth. They have hunted down the remnants of mankind from the four corners of the Earth.

These are the names of the beasts that are lined up ready for battle on the crater's edge, fang and claw glistening ready to drive mankind to his doom; Smilodon, Hyenadon, Enteledont, the great bear Arctura Simus, Andrewsarchus, the dire wolf, Dinotherium and the cave lion. It is a terrible sight, woe to mankind in its last hour, there goes up a cry for help, but no help comes, for when the innocent needed help to protect them from man, no help came to them either, so why should it be any different now? The great beasts salivate with anticipation of the final destruction that they are about to visit upon their victims, and this time they are invincible!

As I read the next few lines I saw the last people ever to walk on the face of the Earth being torn apart by savage beasts. And then the Earth fell silent.

3465AD. The Earth is ravaged by storms and winds and swirling clouds of dust, here and there are the tell-tale signs that mankind once inhabited this planet. The natural world is continuing. Insects and molluscs are growing larger and more varied while jellyfish look set to dominate the seas with newly formed gigantic species.

l looked upon the ghostly form of the monk and said, 'I can't take anymore of this, return me to my body on Earth.'

The spectre turned its head towards me and spoke in a ghastly voice, 'You should not have come here, no one can hear the prophecies and return to Earth, lest the prophecies be made known. Back on Earth your physical body is now in a hospital bed where it shall remain in a coma for the rest of your natural life.'

I screamed at the spectre in total disbelief, '*No, no!*

The spectre replied, 'There are others like you who have been foolish enough to come here through meditation and they also wander the Martian deserts as ghosts.'

I grabbed the spectre by his robe, 'Please don't allow this to happen, I must go back to my body, I have a family, I ... '

Terrified and furious, I grabbed the hood of the robe in order to see the face and then I opened it ... there was only darkness where the head should have been.

The robe fell to the floor as though there had never been anyone in it and immediately the monastery disappeared leaving me trapped forever at the freezing south pole of the planet Mars. The only thing that remained was the distant sound of the spectre laughing.

POETIC JUSTICE
Andy Botterill

'Apply the butter thinly and evenly,' Mother always said. He'd heard her say it a thousand times at least. 'Get it into each corner of the bread.' She was always right. She knew what was what. 'Butter makes the world go round,' She explained. 'It is the very structure and foundation on which this great country was built.' He'd heard her say it many times, but he'd never seen it himself, not the outside that is. This was all he knew - this little piece of Earth. This was his place. He had nothing else.

Apply the butter thickly and evenly, with a knife. He didn't have a knife. He wasn't allowed that. It wasn't safe. He wasn't allowed clothes, let alone something sharp. He couldn't be trusted with anything sharp he might hurt himself with. Apply the butter thinly and evenly, on his hands, and then put them between two slices of bread he'd found in the old barn. That was his home most of the time. Apply the butter, feel it on his skin, all greasy and warm. Put his fingers between the bread and try to eat them. He knew nothing of cannibalism, self harm. It meant nothing to him. He only knew what he'd learnt, within the confines of this limited space. Nothing else mattered. He knew nothing of art, religion, politics. They were alien concepts, from an alien world. They were something else, something else beyond his comprehension, that had no meaning, not to him, not here. They simply didn't count. They were part of a life, a world he had no part of and never would.

Sometimes he was allowed out, out of the barn at least. Sometimes he was allowed out to stretch his legs. Sometimes he was allowed out for a brief walk, like a caged beast given momentary release. Maybe that's what he was. That's what he felt like. Sometimes he could be seen in his swimming trunks, in one of the fields beyond the farm. He could be seen lying in the long grass, his arms stretched out, pretending to swim. He wished he could swim away, swim away to somewhere else, somewhere different. Surely there was more than this, if he could only find it, if he could only escape, but he couldn't. He dare not even try it. He feared the big stick. He feared that most, the big stick she beat him with. If he strayed too far, it was sure to come out. It always had, since he was a kid. He was almost a man now, but he still feared it. It still held him captive. It still had some kind of power over him. It had broken almost every bone in his body that stick had. He had every reason to fear it, and God did she know how to wield it. She was an expert. She knew how to inflict hurt with maximum impact. If he was ever going to escape, he'd have to get it right. There could be no second chances. If she caught him, the stick would come out. He could be sure of that. She'd beat him within an inch of his life, maybe more than that. Maybe she'd actually go the whole way. Perhaps it would be a mercy if she did. Perhaps it would be a mercy if she put him out of his misery. God, did he hate that stick. He imagined breaking it into little bits, burning it perhaps, even turning it on her if he had the strength, but he couldn't. She was built like an ox. A farmer's wife, she was a brute. He had no chance. There was no point even thinking about that. It wasn't an option. She was just too strong for him.

He liked to slither through the grass. It was one of his pleasures in life. He'd seen snakes, slow-worms. He liked to imitate them. He liked to imitate the animals around him. Sometimes he thought he was one of them and not a person. It was only seeing her and recognising some of her in himself that he realised he wasn't. He had two legs and not four. He also had some vague recollections of a sister from the very distant past, but he couldn't quite remember, and his mother never mentioned her. What had become of his sister? Did he really have one? Had he just imagined it all? It was just something deep inside him, locked away in his brain, told him that once as a child there had been playing, even fun, but no more. It had all gone. What had happened? What had gone wrong?

Sometimes he pretended he was a sheepdog. His mother seemed to like that. It seemed to give her some strange pleasure seeing him run round on all fours, barking out loud. She liked that, 'I could use you in the fields,' she joked. 'You could round up the sheep as good as any dog.' Or, 'Be a pig,' she'd suddenly announce. 'I want to hear you oink. I want to hear you squeal.' If it kept her happy, he did it. If it kept her away from the stick and using it, it made perfect sense. It was best to keep on the right side of her if he could. He'd learnt that. It was a mistake to rile her up. It was foolish to cross her. It was a mistake to get her upset. If he did, he knew the price to be paid. He knew what to expect.

She kept him chained up at night, sometimes in the barn, or sometimes in the yard, depending how cold it was. Then she'd go inside and come back with a bowl of food she'd leave out, all scrag-ends and left-overs of course, from something nice she'd had. He ate it just to fill himself up and keep himself alive. Then he'd watch in the dark for an hour or two until eventually the light in the old cottage would go out and she'd go to bed, and he'd be left by himself staring up at the star-filled night, with just his thoughts, wondering if anything good would ever happen, or would it always be like this?

In the morning everything would be the same. It would be just the two of them. Once he'd had a father. He must have done, but he'd gone. What had she done to him? What had she done to everything? Was she a normal mother? Was everyone like her? Were there any others? Was there anyone else, on the outside? Were they alone in the world? Would he ever find out? Would he ever get the chance to live a proper life?

Occasionally she talked of the outside, of shops, towns, other people, but he'd never seen them. He'd never seen them for himself. He only had her word they existed. That's all he had. She could have been making it all up. He wouldn't have known any different. That was until the night when they arrived, they finally came, in a big white car with a flashing blue light on top. Two of them got out, police officers, but he didn't know that. He just watched in stunned silence as they went up to the door of the farmhouse. They knocked, once, twice and eventually she came out. He didn't know whether to be delighted or scared. He was a bit of both.

'What do you want?' his mother scowled in a gruff voice.

'Mind if we have a look about?' said one of the officers who was wearing a tall, blue hat.

'I do mind as a matter of fact,' she said. 'Have you got a warrant?'

'You are Mrs Greenwood, are you not?' the officer continued.

'That's right, so what?'

'Well, we're investigating the alleged disappearance of your daughter Kate and your husband John. Where are your husband and daughter Mrs Greenwood? Are they here?'

'They've gone.'

'Where have they gone?' the officer asked.

'I don't know. I never done nothing to John.'

'And where is your son, Mrs Greenwood?'

'He's here. There's nothing wrong with him.'

'We've had a report you keep him chained up. Is that right?'

'What business is it of yours?'

'My God, look over there. I don't believe it,' the other policeman suddenly blurted out. He was pointing to the shape of a small, teenage boy lying stretched out in the corner of the yard like a dog. The boy had a chain around his neck, which was attached to a post. They hadn't noticed him at first as he was half hidden by the shadow cast by the barn opposite.

'Is that your son?' the officer continued in a voice full of disgust. 'What on earth have you done to him?'

His colleague rushed over to try to release the teenager, who was almost too horrible to touch, all covered in bruises and his own excrement.

'It wasn't my fault. It was all an accident,' his mother protested. 'I didn't mean to kill Kate. I only hit her once or twice. I didn't hit her that hard.'

'What about your husband, Mrs Greenwood? Did you kill him too?'

'I never did. He killed himself. He couldn't live with the truth and I had to keep Mark here in case anyone ever found out.'

At that moment Mrs Greenwood rushed inside. One of the policemen started to follow her, but she came back out almost immediately waving a shotgun menacingly around her head.

'Duck!' the policeman shouted in warning to his fellow officer, as a single shot was fired in their general direction, but with no real sense of accuracy or of whom she was aiming at.

'Keep away. I'm warning you,' Mrs Greenwood threatened. She then turned the shotgun on herself, pushing the barrel into her own mouth and squeezing the trigger. It was all over before either of the policemen could even move to stop her.

They found the key to Mark's padlock in one of her pockets. It was smeared with her blood, but no one seemed to care very much. Sympathy for Mrs Greenwood was in very short supply. It was almost good that it had ended like this, one of the officers commented. It would save the courts a lot of time and expense. She'd got what she deserved, both policemen agreed.

'Come on, son. We'll soon get you cleaned up,' said one of the officers, helping Mark into the back of the police car.

'I just don't understand how she got away with it for so long,' his companion said with a puzzled look on his face.

'Well, it's very remote out here, barely a soul for miles. Maybe it was lucky we got her at all. It was only the odd remark here and there from the occasional chance visitor, postmen and the like, and she didn't have very many of those as you can imagine, but that's what did it. That's what made us suspicious. We might never have known otherwise. She might have got away with it forever, keeping him locked up like that.'

'Well, I suppose we'd better call an ambulance, get her remains cleared up.'

'No, leave it. Let the animals feed on her for a bit. She's been eating them and treating her son like one of them. It's kind of poetic justice,' the officer said with an ironic tone in his voice.

All three watched with a peculiar mixture of horror and delight as the farmyard animals, chickens, ducks, geese and pigs, slowly started to descend on Mrs Greenwood and tuck into the bloody mess that had once been her face. It was an ugly sight, and yet at the same time it somehow wasn't. It was something almost good.

THE LETTER
Yvonne Bulman

As she walked towards the door and bent down and picked up the envelope her heart sank, surely this couldn't be another letter from the solicitor.

Ever since they had put the house on the market it had been one thing after another. The house was a family home, but now that the children had grown up it was just too big for the two of them. The decision had not been taken lightly, they both loved the house and it had so many happy memories, like the time they'd got a new puppy in the winter and spent hours playing with her in the snow. Celebrating birthdays in the garden and in the house, celebrating 'A' Levels and degrees and then playing with the grandchildren. So much happiness. Shelia gave herself a mental shake, 'think positive' she told herself, a smaller property, preferably a bungalow was the ideal choice at their time of life. Colin's health was not all that good now, not since his stroke and she herself had worsening arthritis, she felt despair threatening to overwhelm her. *Oh pull yourself together woman.* She turned the letter over in her hands, scared to open it, afraid of what it might contain.

Since the house had been offered for sale, there had been lots of problems. They'd had lots of viewings but for the first four months there had been no offers and then after four and a half months there had been John Brown's mother. John lived next door but one to them, he'd got four children who terrorised the neighbourhood and then his mother came to stay, she'd seen the signboard and asked if she could view. It had been quite difficult for Colin and Shelia, they didn't like the Browns and normally would have nothing to do with them, but they hadn't felt they could refuse to let his mother view the property, she might want to buy it. As luck would have it, she did want to buy it - or so she said, but when the estate agent had relayed the offer she made, Shelia and Colin had been very insulted - how could she have thought that they would consider £35,000 less than the asking price! But the Browns had expected it to be accepted and when it wasn't they had been very upset, well John and his wife were, if 'Mummy' wasn't living close by they had no baby-sitter and none of the neighbours were very keen, especially with those children.

Then there had been the Smiths, they really liked the house immediately, they'd made a sensible offer which Colin and Shelia had readily accepted, their surveyor had not found anything wrong, the building society were happy and everything was going well. Shelia often saw the Smith family cruising past the house on a Sunday afternoon and she and Colin had found what they thought was their ideal bungalow. They'd gone away on holiday leaving a contact number with Stephen their solicitor, but there had been no alarms, or so they thought. When they returned from holiday there had been an urgent phone message on their answer phone, from the solicitor, just nine days before they were due to complete Mr Smith's buyer had changed his mind! The Smiths had been devastated and so were Colin and Shelia. They had debated taking the house off the market but had decided against it, they still wanted 'their' bungalow and then came the first letter, that was from the estate agent handling the sale of the bungalow, 'it is with regret that we note that you have withdrawn your offer'. Colin and Shelia had been stunned, they hadn't withdrawn their offer but after a phone call it was established that what was really meant was you can't proceed and our client has had another offer. There had been nothing that they could do, with their house unsold they weren't able to proceed.

Now it was October.

'We'll give it to the end of November, then withdraw it until next year,' Colin and Shelia had agreed.

Then suddenly there was Mr and Mrs Boyle. They had come to view the house on a murky Sunday afternoon and they, like the Smiths, had loved the house. They'd got some quite big furniture and the house was just what they wanted, and, they could proceed, they'd got a buyer for their property and were in a hurry to complete, they would like to move in on the 1st of December. Shelia remembered their elation and then their despair, they'd got nowhere to go and only a matter of weeks to find somewhere. Once again Colin and Shelia spent all their spare time trawling estate agents, viewing bungalows and failing to find anything suitable. The hunt continued and just as they were beginning to lose hope, a possibility was found. It was a detached bungalow with three bedrooms and a small garden, in a semi-rural village. The garden was a bit of a disappointment to Colin especially, he'd wanted a big garden, not that he did very much in the garden but he liked the idea of lots of space, but as Shelia pointed out, she did most of the gardening and neither of them were getting any younger and the property itself would be quite big enough for the two of them and allow them spare bedrooms for when the children and grandchildren came to visit. Having decided, they made an offer which was accepted and the sellers were quite happy to move on the 1st December as they were moving into a new property which was standing empty. With December approaching fast Shelia decided it might be safe to begin packing again and selling some surplus furniture. She also resigned from various committees and groups to which she belonged.

Then came the second letter - this time from their solicitor. Mr and Mrs Boyle still wanted to proceed but there were legal problems related to the sale of their own property, something to do with an outstanding charge, it was not known how long it would take to sort it out!

Almost the end of November and back to square one, Shelia could have wept and once again they debated taking the property off the market but Colin had said no, the people they were buying from were not worried, they would keep their word, certainly until the new year, which would give them a chance to find another buyer. Shelia thought the chances of finding another buyer that quickly was remote but she went along with Colin and then at his suggestion she'd gone to spend a few days with her daughter in the hope that a change would cheer her up a bit. Being with Jenny and the grandchildren was distracting - house selling seemed like a bad dream and then less than three days later Colin phoned her and said they'd got another buyer. She couldn't believe it. But after another day with Jenny she'd returned home.

The new buyers were professional people with two young children. She worked part-time while the children were in nursery and he was a doctor. They were in rented accommodation and had to be out by the end of January.

Christmas came and went, and as soon as people were working again their survey had been carried out and now there was this letter, letter number three, it looked very official. She turned it over and over in her hands, then she realised it was only addressed to her, not to both of them, maybe it wasn't about the house. With trembling fingers she began to open the envelope - no she couldn't do it, she put the letter on the side and picked up the kettle and begin to fill it, from the hot tap. Realising what she was doing she banged the kettle down and snatched up the envelope tearing it open and pulling out the enclosed single sheet ... 'Dear Shelia, just a small token of our appreciation for all the years you have given to the WI Committee ...', a smile spread over Shelia's face, at long last the President had mastered the computer but she fervently hoped that future 'official' looking correspondence would cause less angst for the recipient, than it had for her.

When Colin returned home she told him of her scare and he smiled at her and said, 'No need to worry any more, I saw Stephen while I was out, we can go and sign the contract tomorrow. We're moving on the 30th of January.'

'Oh, thank heavens for that,' said Sheila, 'I swear I'm never going to move house ever, ever again.'

THE LATECOMER'S STORY
Ron Whatley

'You're late,' Burt Evans growled as Tom, the canal lock keeper entered the public bar of the Old Grey Mare Inn.

Old Tom, a lean, grizzled man in his sixties, glanced down at his wristwatch, eyes squinting from beneath beetling black eyebrows. His gaze was fierce when he raised his head again and glared at the assembled cronies, Burt in particular. 'It's only eight o'clock,' he grumped.

Flop and Peterkins, who made up a threesome with Burt, were already comfortable round a favoured fireside table. They grinned at each other like a couple of conspiring gnomes, anticipating sparks flying when Burt and Tom got together under the same roof. Burt was a retired canalman while Tom still worked for the Canal Authorities.

Tom, however, walked straight to the bar without further comment. His face was set like granite as he waited to be served.

'You're late Tom,' commented Bill Bailey, the licensee, as he returned from a brief spell in the saloon bar, where a group of young things seemed to be getting high on an assortment of cocktails.

'Just draw my usual and never mind the blathering,' snapped Tom.

'Exactly thirty minutes late, Tom,' Bill went on as he worked the pump lever. He was a well-built, florid faced man, who had been round the tracks of life a few times. He wasn't fazed by grumpy old regulars like Tom.

Tom could hear Peterkins chortling away in the background. 'Anyway, I know I'm late,' he admitted darkly. He took hold of the foaming pint of mild and bitter and 'killed' it with a number of thirsty gulps. 'Another,' he gasped at the astonished Bill Bailey. The brew seemed to have only whetted Tom's raging thirst. He threw some change down onto the counter.

Bill watched wide-eyed as old Tom sank exactly half of the second beer. 'Now I've caught up with the others,' said Tom, licking his lips. He kept hold of his glass and advanced to the table where the other men were seated.

'So, how did you know we were just supping our second round?' Flop asked. He was really curious.

'Lad, when you've worked on the canals for as long as I have, you learn a thing or two,' Tom answered. There was a canny gleam in his steely blue eyes. Peterkins sniggered at the remark but Flop stared back at the lock keeper without comprehension.

'Well, what did delay you Tom?' Burt inquired, adopting a more conciliatory tone of voice.

The lock keeper wheezed as he settled his bones into an empty seat at the trio's table, ritualistically placing his half full glass onto the table. 'It's like this lads,' he began, his eyes darting this way and that, as if to make certain he had the full attention of the other three. Tom was no mean ham when it came to hogging the limelight. 'Shortly before I was due to go off-duty this evening, this feller comes cycling along the towing path; stops right outside my cottage door.

'Good evening,' the guy says.

'How do', says I.

The stranger seemed to take that as some sort of invitation; climbs off his bike and leans it against my garden wall.'

'The cheek of some folk,' Peterkins mumbled without reason. However, the interruption allowed everyone the chance to lift their beer glasses and sup briefly.

'Aye, the cheek,' said Tom, his lips still glistening with the beer droplets. 'Anyway, this feller - by Go... he was a strange one. He was all wrapped up in dirty, waterproofed clothing and he wore an old woolly hat, pulled right down over his ears. Why, with the beard he sported, you couldn't see much of his face at all. Aye, a strange one. And he looked like he'd been living rough a goodly while.'

'How old was this guy?' Flop questioned.

Tom glared at his companion, allowing his lips to droop a little at the corners. 'Thirty to fifty - difficult to tell. I check canal licences not birth certificates,' he growled. He seemed niggled.

The others stared down at their beers. Flop, especially, seemed suitably chastened.

The old canalman continued with his narrative. 'This feller,' he said slowly, 'scrabbled round inside a duffle bag tied behind the saddle of his bike and lifted out one of those little dogs - a chee-wah-wah, I think it was. Then he set the little mutt on the ground ...'

The others perked up. Now they were all ears.

Tom went on. 'This guy tells me that his little dog had spent the last ten miles riding in that bag. He's all so matter of fact, this feller.'

'It looks like it', says I, for the poor little mite is staggering about all over the show, blinking his eyes at the daylight.

'I wonder if you would be kind enough to let me have some boiling water', the stranger says. He dragged out a pint-sized plastic container from the depths of the bag where the dog had been. Then, from a jacket pocket he took out a paper bag containing tea leaves. He put some of the leaves into the canister, which he handed to me. 'And two or three spoonfuls of sugar if you can spare it', says he with a smile.'

'Somebody's shout,' Flop broke in, toying with his empty beer glass. The other three immediately drained theirs.

'It's your turn Flop, you crafty devil,' Tom said with a steely smile.

'And how do you make that out?' Flop questioned in a protesting tone of voice.

'Easy. Who bought the first round?'

'I did,' Peterkins said with a chuckle.

'And the second?'

'Me,' said Burt.

'And I bought two pints when I came in,' said Tom. 'So that makes it your shout.'

'Sounds right,' said Bill Bailey, who had been listening to Tom's logic from behind the bar.

Flop pulled a sour face and reluctantly collected up the empty beer glasses and took them over to Bill Bailey. His wrinkled face wore a bemused expression.

When the glasses had been replenished and ritually sipped by the four men, Bill Bailey chimed up, 'And did you give this character some hot water?' he asked.

'Did I ... of course I did,' Tom bellowed. 'And then the guy has the cheek to ask for something to eat as well.'

'Cheek of some folk,' Peterkins gurgled.

'Cheek, aye. But I could see he was hungry so I rummaged round in my place and found three bananas and several slices of bread. He ate that like he was starving. Not the mutt though; wouldn't touch any of the titbits I offered it - even some old bits of cheese and some crumbs of meat that had been leftover from lunch.'

'So, what happened next Tom?' Bill Bailey had become so intrigued in the tale that he was neglecting other customers.

'Well, after this chap had eaten, he tells me his name is John Mallet. He reckoned he travelled up and down the canal system regularly every year.

'Do you?' says I, because I've lived round these parts for thirty odd years and I've never laid eyes on this feller before.

'Oh yes. Canals are my hobby. I once helped out on a voluntary dig on the Avon Canal', he said.

'Did you?' I said, thinking that the Avon is a goodly distance away from my patch on the Grand Union Canal.

'Yes', he said. 'I'm a carpenter by trade. But right now I'm looking for a cottage and two or three acres of ground'.

You'll be lucky, I was thinking.

'Yes, I'd really get organised', says this Mallet. 'Be self supporting - chickens, goats. Positive thinking, that's what some of you canal people could do with.' Tom pursed his lips. This Mallet feller was beginning to annoy me.

'You could do all this with some chickens and a goat?' I asked.

'That and a bit of determined effort - helping to get the canals working usefully again', Mallet says. 'With respect, sir, you canal people are a bit on the thick side'.'

The lock keeper took a sip from his beer. 'By this time I was really fed up with the conversation. Besides, I was off-duty. So I shut up, hoping he'd take the hint and leave.' Tom paused, thinking back. 'Well, by and large, he did go; scooped up that poor chee-wah-wah, put it back into his duffle bag and climbed aboard his bike.

'You did say you've travelled these parts before?' I thought to ask him, as he started to cycle off along the towpath.

'Many times', he called back.'

Tom nodded his head sagely. 'I'm thinking, good luck then, because he's sure to know all about the deep pot holes ...'

A pregnant silence followed while Tom drained his glass.

'Is that all there is to tell?' Burt wanted to know.

Tom ignored the question. 'Your shout Peterkins,' he declared ruthlessly.

Peterkins rose from his seat like a man who had been hypnotised. He wandered across to the bar and threw some money down on the counter and Bill Bailey began pulling fresh pints.

'Elixir of life,' Tom commented when he had sampled his drink.

'A rum old story you tell,' Burt said.

'Rum, aye. And so was Mallet,' Tom said. 'He made quite a splash when he tumbled into the canal, I can tell you.'

'He fell in?' Bill Bailey questioned.

'Aye, of course he did: he hit one of those pot holes and went base over apex into The Cut - bike as well. That's why I was late this evening, had to fish the bugger out; couldn't swim. The dog was okay though.'

'Well, you might have warned this Mallet feller,' Burt admonished crustily.

'Why?' Tom seemed genuinely puzzled. 'He was one of them know-it-alls - he wouldn't have listened to any advice from me. Besides, he coughed up ten quid when I dragged him out of the water.' Tom looked gleeful. 'Strange one, he was. By Go... I bet he was one of those eccentric millionaires you read about ...'

'What I want to know is how you figured we were drinking our second pint when you came in?' Burt said, getting back to a subject that had been bothering him since Tom had joined them.

Tom turned on him. 'Do you think I'm daft lad?' he snarled. 'I was thirty minutes late: your glasses were half empty and Peterkins was giggling his fool head off, like he does after his first pint. And since we haven't been known to down three pints apiece in the first half hour, you three must have been supping your second drinks. Simple deduction lad. Aye, we canalmen might be thick but not that thick.'

Flop thought there was something amiss with Tom's reasoning but his head was too fuzzy to try to fathom it out.

PARTY POOPER
Kathleen Townsley

Was that the alarm? No I was dreaming. Eyes shooting open again, Carol looked at her radio alarm. It was the alarm, and she had slept for a further half hour. 'Not again,' she screamed, 'I am already on my final warning.' Jumping out of bed she ran at full speed down the stairs, dressing as she ran. Grabbing her keys she ran for the bus.

Standing at the bus stop, people stared at her. An elderly man said, 'I have always been known as being liberated but I think you have gone too far this time young lady.' Looking down at herself she screamed and ran behind the bus shelter, remaining there till the bus came and the coast was clear.

How the hell am I to get home? she thought. Even though she could see her home, the street looked ten miles away. The skirt she had picked up was an underskirt. The blouse she had grabbed was see-through and was meant to go over a T-shirt. Her bra was the one without shoulder straps, and not being too well endowed, never remained in-situ. Her knickers were the ones to be thrown out or cut up for dusters as they had been washed by mistake and were now a dirty shade of green. She was wearing one lace-up shoe without the laces and one slip-on loafer, one knee length pop sock, and one leg of a pair of tights, the other tight's leg was blowing behind. Taking off the pop stock she grabbed the blowing tight and climbed into it, doing so, four large ladders ran up the tights, tucking the blouse inside the underskirt she tied the pop sock around her waist to act as a belt, undoing the strapless bra she wriggled out of it and put it back on over the blouse, hoping the material would hold it in place. Nothing could be done with the knickers, the same with the footwear, at least she had managed to cover some of her embarrassment. Peeping round the bus stop she walked towards her street, so far so good, till she reached the first house on the corner. The school bus was picking up the children. Leaping quickly over the small wall into the corner house's garden, she scrambled into the privet hedge, making herself as small as possible she waited for the school bus to pass.

She seemed to have been there for ages when a small dog came sniffing round the hedge, cocking its leg it covered her back in a warm stream of urine, then immediately ran away as its mistress called. Two children then sat on the wall, she knew if they turned round she would be spotted. Trying to breathe quietly she listened to their conversation. Finally they jumped up as the bus approached and threw their yoghurt cartons over the wall, which landed in her lap, and immediately emptied their contents.

After a few minutes she forced herself back through the hedge and climbed back over the wall. As she stepped down she realised her loafer was still in the privet hedge and her bare foot had just settled in a warm doggie poo. Her hair was full of twigs, scratches ran up her arms and the only decent tight was now in shreds. The only good thing was the strapless bra was still in place.

Standing up she started to limp up the street. She had no intention of climbing back over the wall for her loafer. All was going well when she saw her neighbour coming down the street towards her. She was still a fair way off. Carol quickly veered into the alleyway and hid behind the large skip sitting there. Just as she settled into position, she heard her neighbour shout good morning to someone. It did not take long for her to find out who, for a bucket full of plaster waste descended over her head. *Nice shot,* she thought, coughing and spluttering. After a short while she stepped from behind the skip and tried to brush herself down, only to find the dust had adhered itself to the doggie poo and the yoghurt. *At least it covers some of my dignity,* she thought, totally fed up by now. She set off once again to try and make it home. *Surely nothing else can go wrong?* she thought. How wrong can you be?

Keeping as close to the wall as possible, she was making excellent progress, concentrating on not being seen. Mistake. She stood in another doggie poo. She said out loud, 'Have these people never heard of poo scoops?' only to jump when a voice said.

'Pardon dear?'

Turning slowly she saw an old lady peeping through the hedge. Quickly she scurried away before the old dear got a good look. She could see her beautiful front door coming nearer, limping along even faster she stopped dead. Her boss was knocking on her front door. *Oh no,* she thought, then she smiled. *Well at least this time he can see why I am late,* she thought, and pushing her shoulders back she marched through the garden gate, arriving at her door, just as her boss was turning to leave. His jaw dropped and he looked at her. 'Well Carol, I was prepared to give you the benefit of the doubt, but here I find you coming home at this time of the morning after a night on the tiles. Sorry Carol but you are sacked. Collect your wages and cards tomorrow.'

'Too late,' said Carol, 'I bloody resign.' And rushing past him went inside her house and slammed the door in his face.

Following a hot bath she collected her clothes she had placed in a plastic bag and had a bonfire in her back garden. Smiling she said, 'Maybe I could apply for a job as a spy for I made it safely home unseen, even the best of spies could not do that.'

Settling down in her chair that evening she turned to her favourite page of the evening paper and her favourite reporter, who had been complaining on the Friday evening that due to the flu epidemic he had to work late and was missing a funky party. He had told the readers that he would tell them of his night all alone at the newspaper office, in the Monday evening addition. As she turned to the page her mouth dropped open, for the headlines read, 'If this is the result of the party, then I am glad I did not go'. The rest of the page consisted of a blown up picture of Carol climbing over the wall, for the third time that day Carol screamed.